Legend of the
Knight Saga:
The Chronicles

Legend of the Knight Saga: The Chronicles

Sushrut Tewari

PARTRIDGE
A Penguin Random House Company

To order additional copies of this book, contact
Partridge India
000 800 10062 62
orders.india@partridgepublishing.com

www.partridgepublishing.com/india

Contents

This story is not for the faint of heart. Don't read it. It will be best not to get into such story. I am warning you as I know that once you start reading it, then there is no turning back. You will be hooked with it. So it's better not to read something which might prove to be hazardous for your health.

My name is Nikita Mehra, I am a normal fifteen year old teenager, or should I say, 'I was' before the fateful day, that changed my life. I never wanted to be a princess, I never wanted to be rescued by a prince charming, heck I stopped believing in fairy tales when I was seven years old, all I just wanted was to be a normal teenager.

Then suddenly, earth was in great danger, a kind of danger that no one could solve, so it became my responsibility to protect the earth, and the worst part, everyone expects me to stand up to it!! I never had many friends but now most of the time; I am being protected by my bodyguards that have extraordinary super power! If you're reading this and believe in fairy tales or science fiction containing monsters or wizards or dragons, then close this book, you don't have the slightest idea of what grave problems it can do to you.

If you are hell bent on reading it, and if you find that you have the same thinking as I do, then a word of advice, Close It! And before you know it, you might be thrown into different dimensions and have to stop the evil from destroying the space time continuum kind of crap.

But if you're a normal teenager, (like I was once) then be my guest, open the book and read on, and trust me, if you hope that you are going to be safe, then cross your fingers as this will be one of the most fascinating tale about a journey you've ever read.

Chapter 1

Encountering a Demon-wolf

The exciting and the most horrible part of my story started about ten days ago, in my class....

"So what do you mean by an oxidizing agent, class?" my chemistry teacher asked the whole class full of students.

'Ok, let me guess' I thought, 'they are the substances that remove hydrogen and add oxygen, right. Wait, what if it is the other way around?'

"Come on class," our teacher said "At least try!" My mind started thinking useless things, 'what if I am wrong? The whole class will laugh at me, I can't take that risk, but why can't I answer the silly question, my memory can't be that bad' and then I sighed 'Yes, my memory *can* be that bad'

"No one?" she asked "does no one wants an 'A' grade?" and before the word 'grade' was finished only one hand in the whole class was raised. It was Madhav, he stood up and said "Ma'am, oxidizing agents are those substances which remove hydrogen and add oxygen" he then balanced his specs as a sign to show that he was absolutely right.

It all ended when our teacher gave him an 'A' in his response, and ordered the whole class to clap for him. I cursed myself, even though I knew the correct answer, I still hesitated in answering it! In the gloom I started talking to myself, (I do this a lot when I am angry). Unfortunately the teacher caught me, and said "Nikita my dear, can you balance this equation?" she said pointing at the black-board.

I know all about the 'Nikita dear' crap. She always does this whenever she finds me talking to myself (which, according to her is 'disturbing the class'). Managing to stay calm, I went towards the black board. 'I wanted to answer the other question, not this one!' I thought. I just kept the edge of the chalk on the black-board, praying to god that I at least understand the question!

It didn't take long for our teacher to realize that I did not know anything. She said "Get back to the chair dear, and please pay attention!" as I went back; I saw at least dozens of faces that had a smile showing their prejudice. And among them was the face of my two friends Amrit and Jyoti!

"You made your self look like a fool!" Said Amrit, "Yeah" Jyoti chimed in, "I could have answered that one very easily". Meet my two friends, Amrit Sharma and Jyoti Riana. They are what I call 'friends'

Jyoti is a very talkative girl in the class, who has beauty, but no brains; she hardly pays any attention to studies, and spends most of the time gossiping around. Then comes Amrit. He is our school's hockey captain. He is a tall, strong, and quite smart. Apart from being nosy, he is the only boy whose feminist thinking matches with mine.

Our teacher then called Madhav, who without wasting another second, balanced the equation as if it was child's play for him. Madhav Verma, our school's best and brightest. His I.Q is over one hundred and forty-nine. Ask him anything, and I mean, anything, and he will answer it in a jiffy! He talks less, and his voice is only heard when there is an answer he has to say. He wears round specs, which resembles a lot like of 'Harry Potter'

After the incident, the usual things started happening, in each period, Madhav would answer something, and would get another 'A', while my useless brain would wandering in its own world. This is why my friends and relatives call me immature, but I don't find it too problematic, I mean, this is the age to think, right? After growing up, no one will remember what kind of things they used to think while they were teenagers.

After the last lecture, we all packed our bags. Just as I exited the class room, I heard some noises and screams coming out of my class. As I turned back I saw that Madhav had got in a fight! This was a bad call for him, because he can't save his butt. And this time, he was in big trouble, he pissed of Vishal Gulati, our schools sports captain, and boy did he kill him.

Gulati almost killed Madhav till Amrit came in between, all the class was laughing at the poor guy, and every one left one by one after watching Madhav getting beaten. I was the only one in the whole class who helped him in getting back on his feet. I could see tears rolling down from his eyes as he took his cracked specs and wore them once again. I helped him in settling his books, and after this we went on.

This is the only good character in me; I like to help people no matter what others think about me. He stood up and thanked me graciously, and then we both started walking to the gates of the school.

"You're the first person ever to help me like this Nikita" he said, "I just hope not the last"

"Oh no," I replied trying to make him feel better, "You'll have lots of friends one day, people just have to see the world as you see"

"You don't understand Nikita"

"What?"

"You don't understand but you will that I am the last person in the whole school to hang out with"

I couldn't understand what he meant, but something else, something extraordinary, got my attention. I saw a person, with a white colored helmet was looking at me from the window. His helmet resembled the one of a power ranger, just a transparent glass was where there was supposed to be a Black one.

I could see his eyes. He was looking at me, with such a gaze, as if he was protecting me, like a hawk or an eagle, and on my each step, he would shiver. The most astonishing part was that no one saw him! One student was just in front of him, but didn't even bother to look at him, and another one was looking at him as if he was looking right through him.

Another thing was the most peculiar. Our school was having 4 floors, and we were on the third one! There was no way anyone could climb the wall like this guy. There was no ladder, no rope, and I knew that there was no way our school would let anyone do this kind of stunt like the nut was doing.

I tapped Madhav's shoulder and whispered "someone is watching us" he glanced at the window and said "What are you saying, I can't find anyone!" when I looked back at the window, then there was no body.

'Ok Nikita' I thought, 'You're hallucinating baby. You've got to control your useless brain or you'll end up in a mental asylum! But I knew that I clearly saw someone, or maybe it was just a figment of my imagination? Maybe I am a little bit immature, maybe the elders are right' I was so confused in my own emotions that I couldn't see that Madhav was watching me acting so weird.

"Are you ok?" he asked me.

"Oh yes, totally fine" I replied

"You sure?"

"You bet" I answered. Then as we reached at the gate, Madhav took his school bus while I started walking on the pavement. My house was not even a kilometer far from the school. I was walking but my mind still wavered as I could not forget the about the picture of the person. I tried to forget about him but it was like imprinted on my head. Whenever I closed eyes, then the picture of the mysterious person would flash in my mind. But as I moved on, I started thinking about other things.

The hot sun was making the weather so uncomfortable, that I wished to Jump inside a pool full of freezing water. It was a sticky July evening. So I had thought that it would be warm, but not this much! I saw a passerby pouring water over his head; another one was flapping a newspaper to cool himself down. The babies of a mother were crying as she tried to keep them and herself cool by using a battery powered mini fan.

It was so hot that I felt everything will melt; I wanted to buy some ice-cream and slam it on my face just for the sake of cooling me down. I had seen news that the weather would be at its pinnacle of temperature, but somehow, I thought that the worst was yet to come (I hate myself when I am right).

Suddenly, I heard barks of a dog, when I looked back then I saw a street dog glaring at me while barking. It made me feel uneasy, you know, I have a history with dog attacks, a couple of years before It was Holi (festival of colors), when I threw a water-balloon on a street dog (though my intention was to hit another girl), he left me at that time, but made my life hell for the rest of 3 months. He would chase me when I was going back to my house from school I had to ask papa to bring me from home to school and vice versa. A couple of years earlier too, when I was

9 years old, then we visited a neighbor, who had a Pomeranian, at the first site, he bit me, (for which his master call it 'love') and a couple of years earlier too.... Oh, you get the idea.

The barking of the street dog made me feel uneasy. For a few minutes, he followed me barking all the way. The people passing by were getting irritated from the dog too. I wanted to throw a rock on him, but due to my past experiences, I stopped.

To avoid him, I took a shortcut. I went through the park, as it had saved me a couple of minutes of journey. This dog was now pissing me of; I didn't know what it wanted from me. I tried to think about something else, so I looked in up, in the air, this would always get me distracted whenever I felt bored.

Up there, I saw two birds soaring in the air, flapping their wings. But there was something different, the speed of their flapping wings was decreasing periodically, but they were not coming down. This continued until, they just paused in midair! They were still. When I looked around then I realized, that everything was paused! Except for me and the dog, everything became stiff! Everything, people, birds, cars, animals, even the wind had stopped blowing! It was like someone took a universal remote and paused the whole world!

Suddenly, someone from behind said in Scottish accent, "Don't be astonished lass"

I gazed back but there was no one! Just as I turned once again, I heard the same sentence! But this time, I couldn't believe my eyes, the stray dog opened his mouth and said "yes, I said this, what, ye never seen a Demon-wolf before?"

I somehow managed to say "But you're not a wolf, and how can you talk like that!"

But he only replied, "Me lass, if ye is shocked to see this wee thing, then I reckon what you will do when I transform!" and as he finished his sentence he gave a squeal of pain, yet laughed like a maniac! His white fur (or hair) became dark grey. He gained thrice as much size in just one minute. His jaws, his teeth became larger; he was now standing on two feet.

His front paws were transformed into hairy fingers with large claws, his ears became straight and pointy, his eyes were like wild yellow, and the most astonishing part, and he was still going bigger! Where was supposed to be a mere stray dog, there was now a 6 foot tall hungry looking Werewolf with Rabies!

"What do ye think of that!" he said. His yellow hungry eyes were locked on to mine.

"Don't just stand there lass, run. I am here to hunt ye! Now what fun will me get if the prey is so easy to find?" on this sentence, I ran as fast as I could. (Now, I know that it may be a little out of the box for you, but tell me what you will do if you are being hunted by a Werewolf!) I was running so fast that I could hardly breathe. Behind me, I could hear the howl of the wolf. He was laughing while hunting me down.

But luckily, to make it more exciting, he stopped probably trying to play 'Hide and Seek' with me. Being in a park proved to be lucky for me. "Tell ye what, to make this easy for ye I will give ye a 5 minutes head start, me lass"

There were many children who were playing cricket (or should I say, supposed to play cricket, as everything was paused.) The cricket ball was in air, I saw that it was about to be hit by the bat, and then it hit me! The Bat!

I grabbed the bat from the kid's hands, and took it with me, to protect myself. And hid behind a bush, but was I late, did the Scottish demon-wolf saw me, I didn't care.

But I could feel his energy, his aura, as he came near. He was sniffing in the air, which was not good; because I know that wolves can sniff blood from even a mile away. He was laughing and sniffing, as he said, "Don't play games with me princess,"

'Princess?' I thought in my mind.

"I know that ye a very easy prey to find." He replied, "I already proved that, so try not to make it more difficult, come out from wherever ye is hiding and I promise that I won't hurt ye, except when I will bite ye and cut ye into pieces!"

He was coming closer to my hideout on each passing second, I held the bat tightly, ready to hit him. I knew that he was just behind me, because I could feel his breath from the bush.

And as he came close, I closed my eyes and, WHAM! I hit him with all my strength that I had in myself, but all I could do was to gaze at him in horror, I knew that I had hit him with everything I had got, but as the bat landed on him, it broke! Yet nothing happened to the wolf!

"Busted!" he whispered to me smiling, "Now that's more like it, I love when the prey tries to fight back"

This was literally not good, I mean I know that I am not a very strong person; I could hardly lift a dumbbell. But this was not possible, I hit him with all my strength even a world heavyweight wrestling champion would have cried after being hit like that. He didn't dodge it, he didn't even seem to be shocked, and all he did was flash a smile.

He turned to me in mad desperation; I ran but tripped and fell. The Werewolf said while approaching at me "Now that's a pity. I had really expected a tough fight from someone who happens to be a successor to the throne, so much for God Save the Queen"

'Successor? Queen?' I had no idea what was he talking about, he clearly had mistook me for someone else, but it wasn't bothering him in the least. "Ne'er tasted Royal blood before!" he said while licking his big teeth, "I hope it will quench me thirst"

'Royal Blood!' I thought.

His big claws came out, as he looked hungrily at me and said "Close ye eyes lass, ye won't be liking this part" and I knew this was it; this was the end of our brave girl. But I had something else in store for me. Just as the big bad wolf leaped to kill me, someone kicked him even before he could touch me.

The kick was so strong that the wolf went soaring in the air and broke some walls of a nearby building. When I saw my savior then I realized that he was the same guy who was spying on me from the window in the school. This time I could see him perfectly.

He was wearing a Power-Ranger helmet, which was of white color. The only difference was that it was of pure white color, and was not having any other fancy stuff like signs or figures. The helmet was like a mixture of a ninja mask and power ranger helmet. I could see his eyes, as there was only a transparent glass covering that part of his face. He was wearing a black leather-biker jacket which was having a small white colored logo on the right side of the jacket. The logo was of a flying dragon pierced by two swords. Sleek. With black jeans and black pointy-old-man-shoes.

He helped me in standing up. All I could do was to stand there, gazing at the guy and all I managed to ask him was "Who are you?" for which he replied, "You must not ask any question at the moment. For the time being, I am the mysterious warrior"

I was amazed to see such power in a person; clearly he was not from around here. But it was short lived as soon the wolf came back, angrier than ever. When he looked at my savior then he shouted and said "Knight, I have a little proposition to make, why not you take your sorry butt and go back to the silly dimension where ye came from"

"I must say, you have a lot of heart talking to me like that, Can't you see that your enemy is stronger than you? Be gone!" the mysterious warrior shouted.

"Worry not Knight," the Were-wolf shouted, "I am from the Elite degree myself. I'll come after you once I have killed me little prey"

"You shall bring no harm to her, take my word for that"

The Demon-Wolf Growled, and with extra ordinary speed ran towards the warrior as he reached halfway, the warrior started sprinting towards the wolf, and when they came closer, the whole scenario changed. Both of them were fighting, each other with kicks or punches and slashes or bites.

The wolf was trying to bite or cut or slice the warrior, but he would easily dodge his blow, it was as if he was doing something like a daily chore. The warrior, now fully analyzing the technique of the wolf, ran forward and started punching him non-stop. The scenario was sensational, if the whole world could see this than truly we all would have thought that they were superheroes.

With each punch that landed on the wolf's body, I would hear a sound like 'Wham' in the air. His punches were so strong that they were emitting sound-waves in the air. It was A-M-A-Z-I-N-G

He was punching the wolf continuously! But after couple of dozen of punches, the warrior stopped to catch his breath. Using the opportunity, the wolf tried to punch him, but the warrior leaped in the air, swirled, and kicked the wolf so hard that he flew away, this time, on a much greater distance. I saw him breaking a couple of buildings and their walls as he vanished away in the rubble, and I could see him no longer.

All I could say was "T-T-The w-w-wolf?" as the warrior came near me, I moved back. On watching my reaction, he said "Rest assured my lady; the beast shall harm you no more". He was having a kind of British accent, but I knew that I had heard that voice before, one too many times! And I had also seen his eyes, but I couldn't recall it where or when, but in a way, he seemed to be a friend with whom I had shared all my childhood.

I was just about to ask him like 'Where are you from?' but instead of this, only a three letter word came out of my mouth, and that was B-U-S, and I shouted "Watch out, here comes the BUS!!!!"

The wolf, which was still alive, threw a big bus right at us, but thanks to the warrior that he saw it coming in time, and ran towards the upcoming bus, he braced for impact, and grabbed it with his two bare hands!

The impact force was so much that he was still being dragged by the bus; luckily, he was able to stop the bus just before it touched me. He then lifted the bus on his hands, and jumped for the wolf. Just as the wolf came back, the warrior greeted him by smashing the bus right on top of him, crushing the wolf's body, and entombing him. After this, he jumped on the ground

But what followed next was really extraordinary. The wolf still hadn't given up. He lifted the crushed bus, swinging it, and hit the warrior so hard that this time he went away flying in the air. But it didn't take long for him to gain balance. He stopped his flying body by the help of a tree, and ran towards us.

But I realized that he couldn't reach in time, I was sure of it, because he had to cover over forty feet to get to me, while the wolf here was just 9 feet away.

The wolf looked at me and said "So lass, where were we?" he approached at me slowly and slowly, I wanted to run, but I was so terrified that I could hardly say anything. He came closer to me, opened his big jaws, and growled. Just as I tried to bit me, the warrior somehow managed to jump on the wolf, and saved me. They once again started there brawl, but this time, the wolf had an advantage. He was sitting over the lying warrior.

He tried to scratch his helmet, but to my surprise, no harm came to it. Whenever, the wolf tried to scar it, the scratch would itself vanish just as fast as it came. Nothing could happen to it, his helmet was intact, not even a little scratch. But I was more worried for the warrior than his helmet. The wolf was now punching him, and definitely enjoying it. With each punch that would land on his face, the ground below it cracked. And after a couple of punches, he created a kind of a big hole on the ground

The warrior was trying desperately to stop him, but the wolf was defiant, it was either him, or his death. They both were punching each other, but the wolf was gaining the upper hand now. The warrior was now tired. He tried to get up, but the wolf kicked him so hard that the ground broke down.

"So knight? Any last words?" the wolf asked, after being ready to make its final attack. But to this, the warrior replied, "Yes" and just as the wolf could bite him, he leaped forward and grabbed its massive jaws. They both dropped down, the wolf started rolling so that the warrior would leave him. But he didn't.

The warrior stretched and stretched and in the end said "the last word that you will listen demon, is this," and then he shouted "RA-ZE-KA-HE-SH0-YAZ!" and with this, he stretched the wolf's jaws so much that it broke. And the wolf dropped down dead. But this was not enough for the warrior, just as he stood up, the warrior snapped it's neck, and broke it. This time, when the wolf lifeless body fell down, it started to change.

Within a minute, the wolf's body started transforming into a statue, and then it became dust; it flew as the wind blew it away. The warrior closed his eyes for ten seconds, as if mourning for his dead enemy, and then turned to me.

And me, I could hardly do something, it felt as if my own mind was shut down, or my nervous system was still buffering due to the action I just saw.

"Is your ladyship ready? He asked me while bowing down as if he had just met queen of England.

"Ready, for what?" I blurted out.

"Is your highness ready for the transportation through the portal?"

"Portal, what kind of portal, portal to where?"

"To Galdarth milady," he continued, "We must make haste, there is not much time"

"I don't understand we don't have much time for what, what is going to happen?"

"The destruction of your dimensional planet, earth milady, Earth"

Chapter 2

Zapped from Earth!

I would love to tell you how awesome it felt at that time, but as I don't want to completely ruin the tale so...

"Destruction of earth!" I shouted at him. At that time I really had thought that this guy was crazy! There was no way that I could believe in such kind of crap. I mean, I do understand that our earth is on the verge of destruction due to global warming, but this, this was completely of the charts.

"Yes Milady" he continued, "I am speaking of the inevitable destruction of your precious earth."

"No, this isn't happening" I shouted, and pinched myself, so that if it was a dream (more likely a nightmare) then I could open my eyes, but no. "I can't believe this, you're not true, and I am dreaming, you're just a figment of my imagination, my miserable yet awesome action packed imagination!"

"Really if you think so, then please do tell milady," he said after getting on his feet, "About ten minutes ago you wouldn't believe in a werewolf, yet here you are still alive after having a near death experience from a monster similar to a werewolf. A monster called the 'Demon-Wolf'"

He got me, but still being stubborn I asked him "That must be one of my dreams too, I am a day dreamer, yes right, I must be sleeping, and this can't be true."

The masked warrior was now losing his temper, he said "Milady, don't act as if this is all a game, the responsibility of both your world and mine, is on your shoulders. And if you still want to see the proof, then I would advise you to look at your sun, right now!"

I did what he told me to, and all I could do was gaze at our sun with horror. The sun was totally red, giving out red colored radiations and covering our surrounding in light red/orange color. It was thrice as much big, as if it was about to burst, I could see little eruptions of lava and huge, blasts of fire on its surface. And it took me some time to realize, that the weather was going warmer. Within a minute, the sun had transformed into that massive ball of radiations.

"To prevent the destruction of your earth, your family, your loved ones, you must undertake a dangerous journey, full of perils and dangers Milady." He said.

"What if I say no?" I asked him still glaring at the colossal sun.

"Then I fear, that no one will be able to save both of our planets" he said

"Even if you are right, and this isn't a geographical problem, I still don't understand what it has got to do with me!" I exclaimed.

"Rest assured your highness, all your questions will be answered soon, if you come with me" he replied

I didn't want to believe what he was saying; I could bet that I was not the solution to this kind of grave problem. But what if he is right, what if he really needs me, what if in reality the responsibility of billions of lives were on my shoulder, I just couldn't ignore it. But was I up for it?

"I need some time to think for it" I said

He immediately bowed down and said "With all due respect your highness, time is of the essence."

"Don't Bow down, and look I don't even know, if you're right, I only want twenty four hours, I can even come before the allotted time, and you must meet me here on the same place where we are standing ok? And then I'll tell you my conclusion" I said. I wanted him to agree, but I hoped that it didn't piss him of.

He looked a little tensed but then he said "Your Excellency is most right, one must take a few hours rest before taking such a perilous journey from which no one has ever returned—I mean no one has ever tried."

"Did you just said 'No one ever returned'" I asked glaring at him,

"No I said no one has ever tried." he said gulping down

"No you said 'No one ever returned'"

"No I didn't!"

"Yes you did"

"No" he replied, but after realizing that he was outwitted, the warrior said, "so the morrow my lady." He bowed down and ran and ran until he vanished after turning on a street.

And then as I blinked my eyes, everything came back to normal, but the only difference was, that there was no crushed bus, no broken houses, and no broken trees.

The only thing that made noise was of the boy from which I borrowed the bat. He actually fell down for a count when he swings his empty hands.

For a few seconds, I couldn't even believe what happened with me. But then as I looked up in the sky, I realized that this all was true. The sun was literally looking as if it was going to burst any second! But I couldn't imagine that how could all this happen, just in one second.

Apart from me, now there were loads of people who were looking at the giant sun. Some were clicking its photos, others were calling their family to see the drastic changes in the sun, and the rest of them were just gazing at it in astonishment.

Though I had realized that it 'may' have something to deal with me, but it still couldn't answer some of my questions like why did the Were-Wolf called me 'queen' or saying that I have 'Royal Blood' or why did the Mystical warrior bowed in front of me.

I somehow managed to reach my house, while looking out for every stray dog that looked.........a little different

Finally when I got home then I took a breath of relief, '500 meters and no Demon-wolf till now, good enough' and as I entered, I once again became a normal teenager.

"How was your school?" My mom asked, for which I replied 'ok' my mother is a librarian in a private school. She has those one of the calm behavior just like any other librarian. But I think that I am just the opposite. I FREAK OUT totally sometimes, especially during surprises (which kind of happened with me today)

I wanted to go to my room, but there was only one thing that caught my eye. My dad was watching news on the latest documentary of the SUN.

I stood there glaring at the T.V as the reporter said "The scientists have confirmed that this is the Red Giant stage of our Sun. One of the last phases of a dying star. After the Red giant stage, a colossal blast termed as a Supernova will take place, which may result in total destruction of earth. Still the question is that how could mankind exist due to this dramatic change of the Sun. Will we perish, or will we manage to survive this. The question will remain unanswered for now."

Watching the documentary, I ran towards my room. And for the rest of the day, all I did was to stare at the sky and the big red sun. My mind was spinning as I could not decide what to do. I had millions of questions, and not even a single answer. I thought for hours on this matter, and I was so engrossed that I didn't even change my school clothes.

I couldn't even ask something from my parents like "Hey Mommy, I was just saved by a mysterious warrior from being killed by a Demon-wolf. And in this whole wide world only I am supposed to stop the destruction of earth. But for that I have to opt for a very dangerous journey, can I please?" no this won't help, not one bit.

So I was on my own. I was so tensed that I even refused to take dinner when my mother called me. To calm myself down I went to sleep. This is what I do when I have a major problem to solve.

Though, it was not even eight 'o' clock, still to bring my mind to ease I closed my eyes and slept, that too with my dirty school clothes on!

I had a dream. In the dream I saw that I was standing with all the people that I love, my parents, my cousins, my friends, relatives, and even my boring school teachers.

We all were having a very happy time. Laughing, cracking up jokes, or playing. But suddenly, some of them started to change. And to my horror they were changing in stones, and statues, just the same like the werewolf.

There laughter turned to cries and wails. They all were calling me for help. But I couldn't do anything. It was a miserable sight.

As I blinked my eyes, I realized that the world is finished, and I am surrounded by piles of the corpse of humans, and their skeletons.

I woke up from the nightmare. And I knew what I had to do. It was selfish on my part not to heed the gravity of the warrior. I should have gone when I had a chance, now I am thinking about my mistake at two 'o' clock in the morning!

Without wasting any other second. I leaped out of my bed, and the first thing that I did was to get my schoolbag. I emptied it, and stuffed it with clothes, and a towel. I added my tooth brush, soap, and an 'Archie's: Betty and Veronica' comic book.

I changed my clothes, and put on a track suit, my sneakers, and my cap. And I also took my MP3 player with me. I tip-toed down stairs, and slowly went to the fridge without being noticed.

I opened my fridge and made at least a dozen of sandwiches as I didn't know how long the trip would take. It took me at least four lunchboxes to squeeze my sandwiches. And then I stuffed my lunch boxes in my bag.

I made a list of the things I took for my journey. Like

1) Woolen/winter clothes: check
2) Enough food to last at least for a week: check
3) Summer clothes: check
4) Extra pair of socks: check

And a couple of other things that I'll need for the journey. And after packing my bag, I was ready, ready for my most Memorable-terrifying-awesome-dangerous kind of journey. I was ready.

I somehow managed to get out of my house without being noticed by someone. I walked till I reached the park where I first met the Warrior. It was three in the morning, and the weather was a little cold.

Though I am not allowed to go outside after nine, but in this case, I had to make it an exception. I sat on a bench, and waited for the warrior at least next fifteen minutes. And then I realized my stupidity, we had fixed a different time for the meeting!

In total dismay, I started going back; suddenly I heard some noises from the park. It was the guard, and this time I was in real mess. And he was not alone; there were 3 more guys with him. I tried to hide but he pin-pointed the flashlight on my face, and shouted, "Who's there!"

Great, end of the journey before it has even begun, that's my luck. And there was no way I could explain my reason to them, they won't even believe it for a second. And I didn't know why, but I had pictures in mind where I was taken a prisoner in my own house, and I was so old and weird. I was grounded till I turned 101 years old! But thank god as it was only my imagination.

"What are you doing here?" he asked me, for which I just kept my mouth shut, then he asked me, "At least say your name", this time I answered his question, and telling him my name (which seems to be very normal) was my greatest mistake.

As I told them my name, all of them started looking at each other, and grinned. "I am sorry, but you have to come with us" he said, and grabbed me. Others were laughing as if they were some kind of villains in an old movie.

His grip was so strong that it could break my hand. Till the time I saw the problem, it was too late. I saw that the rustling sound of trees were stopped, the there was no voice anywhere. Everything felt the same when the Demon-wolf showed himself for the first time.

I realized that I have to save myself, or these guys will do something horrible, because, they don't feel........... Human. I managed to get free from the guards hand, which made him damn angry.

"What do you think you're doing!" he said, and another one added "Yeah, where do you think you're going?"

"Away from you guys!" I shot back. And then it hit me, when I saw a cat, which was jumping from a wall, it stopped in mid-air! Just like when the werewolf attacked me, the only thing that could move were the four guys, and me.

I knew something was going around here, and somehow I managed to blurt out, "Who are you?" on this question, all of them flashed a smile at me and said "You are about to see it your highness, and sorry for your death,"

"Why, are you apologizing, for my death?" I asked them

"We are because it will soon be taking place." And then another one added, "By our hands that is"

Upon his word, all of them began to change, their skin started becoming light blue, their hair became orange, they gained at least two hundred kilos in just 3 minutes, and their arms were now so big and muscular that it could make a body builder look like a little kid.

They were so big that their clothes were torn of (no, not the undergarments, just the shirts). Their upper body was a little bigger than their legs, so they were walking with little bending down just like a gorilla.

And they all, after being fully transformed, started looking at me, with their green bulging out eyes. They all looked just alike; the only difference was there shirt color, (that was almost torn to bits.)

"What are you guys?" I wailed,

"WE," they all shouted together, "WE ARE THE OGRES!!!" They had a very menacing smile; I could see their, bad black and brown colored teeth.

"What do you want from me?" I shouted in desperation. They all started laughing like a bunch of bozos and then said "Look's to me that your warrior, didn't gave you any memo, We, just like the failed demon-wolf are here to hunt you down."

Another one said "Yeah to kill you," and another one said "to tear ye' to pieces" and another one chimed in "To rip you apart!"

"But" one of them (and probably their leader) said "though we were supposed to kill you right on the spot where and when we see you, but we four brothers, have decided to act otherwise"

"So, you'll let me go!" I thought just as a small light of hope filled my heart with joy.

"No," he said and continued "We all brother's have voted to eat you!!" and once again, they all started laughing. That was very stupid, and horribly disgusting. I tried to run, but as those ogres were having big and strong legs, they easily caught up with me.

They all cornered me, and I was so scared that I could have chewed my nails of! But we had four stupid ogres to do the job. Their leader grabbed me, and placed me on his shoulder. They all were mumbling about how they will start their delicious meal, like here's what I remember,

1: skinning alive
2: roasting on the fire place
3: adding salt and pepper according to the taste
4: serve hot on a plate with an apple in the mouth.

"Let me go!" I shouted, "Put me down!"

"Oh we will put you down, on the fire place!" one of them shot back, "and stop shouting, you're making your throat even more sore, firstly, we don't like our meals having sore throat, and second, no one is going to hear you, no one will help you!"

"Beasts, that's where you are wrong," someone shouted from behind. As I lifted my head, and all of them turned to see, my happiness knew no boundaries, it was the same warrior who saved me from the werewolf!

"Put her Majesty down at once, so then you may avoid tackling the wrath of an Elite knight!" he continued.

"Come on brothers" one of them whispered, "We'll get him, and after killing him we'll get twice as much food!"

But another one contradicted by saying "Have you lost your mind!"

But the first one replied "we don't have a mind!"

Then he said "Oh sorry, I forgot that. But there is no way that we stand a chance, he's one of the Elites, and whereas we are just four 3rd category bounty hunters, he'll finish us in no time!"

Just as when I thought that they will surrender, their leader said "Leave that to me brothers." He placed me down, and went forth "Knight, now, I may not be as learned Galdarthian as you, but I know that you and the warrior's from your kin, are bounded by the act of chivalry."

Now I could see the tension in the eyes of the knight, he was well assured that whatever was coming for him, he wasn't prepared for it. Then the ogre continued "Now, if I reckon correctly, then you are not supposed to use your powers in another dimension, until and unless, you're attacked by another Galdarthian in the same dimension, aye?"

(Now guys, don't get confused, I promise you that I'll clear everything, just hang on to the story please!)

"Well in that case my friend" he said "I don't suppose that you have any right to stop us, so then, we bid you Adieu, and I suppose we're done here?"

They all then looked at me, and flashed me a cunning smile, and then again cornered me. That made me feel really scared, I tried to kick one ogre, but he didn't even feel it.

The eldest ogre was about to lift me once again when the warrior said "Now beasts, who said that only I in the whole world, have the authority to protect her majesty?"

As he finished his sentence, I started hearing the sound of............ hooves! As if a very mighty Steed was coming in this direction to trample us. The sound increased, and through the dark street, I saw a figure of a horse, at some point, when he was visible to all of us, he stopped, and the rider, got down.

He was wearing a long leather cape, black suede shoes, black shirt, attached to the cape, he had long jeans, and in a way, he resembled an eighteenth century warrior or more likely the Count Dracula. His entry in the scene gave me Goosebumps. He was a Six foot tall killing machine!

There was just one thing that made my eyes go wide, and made me hurl my lunch (which I controlled) that thing shocked all of us, except for the warrior. The problem was that he had no HEAD!!!!! Literally, where was supposed to be his head and neck, there was nothing! So he was a six foot tall killing machine with no head!!!

He was having way cool weapons, like two swords, one strapped on his back, and the other on his left side, an axe, strapped right side, and couple of daggers. He was also having another weapon, which was carried around by his Horse; it was a long Whip, which was made by the back bone a human! Yuck!

"Meet the Headless Horseman," the warrior said, "The guardian of her majesty in this dimension!" all I could think was 'I have my Own Guardian, so cool! My own headless horseman!' (Believe me, when you see a werewolf and a couple of ogres in real life, then muttering sentences like these won't bother you in any way)

"I shall not lose to a guy who has no head! Brothers, bring the crossbows!" said the leader ogre, they all slammed their fists on the ground, and made a huge crack, and then took out huge crossbows, each for an ogre. They all pulled the triggers, and started shooting out arrows just like a machine gun.

The horse man dodged some of the arrows by doing acrobatics, and managed to reach his horse. He snatched his whip, and then came forward. When the arrows had finished, then the ogres, took out another clip of arrows. All the ogres reloaded the arrows and started shooting once again, but this time the Horseman was ready!

They all once again started shooting arrows but the horse man used his whip to defend himself. He started rotating his whip so swiftly that it deflected all the arrows. This all continued for a couple of minutes and then when all the arrows were finished, then they tried to reload it, but they had no more arrows. So, they all started sprinting forward to kill the horse man, except for the leader.

The horse man ran taking one of his double edged swords. Just as one of the ogres leaped at him, the horseman dodged him, swirled his long sword, and sliced the ogre, in half. Before the ogre could even realize what happened to him, he broke down to dust.

The second one, tried punching him, but he easily sliced of his hand by using his axe, the hand broke and went to pieces as he reached the ground. And the right next second, he slammed the Axe hard on the head of ogre, and it broke down. The third ogre, who was quite afraid, started shivering in fear! The horse man went slowly towards him, and somehow, when the ogre tried to kick him, the horse pierced his sword right through his chest, and the ogre went to pieces.

Watching all his comrades' die in such a horrid way, (even for an Ogre) the last ogre, who was the leader, started running away! (So much for the leader) but before the leader could escape, the warrior blocked his way and said "Going somewhere"

The Ogre, Punched him so hard that the Warrior fell down, cracking the earth's surface, but the warrior started laughing, and said "Oh no, what have you done now, tried to kill a Galdarthian like you!, and do you know the punishment!" the ogre realized his grave mistake and shouted "Damn you Knight!" he tried to grab him but the Warrior dodged him and Gave such a strong uppercut that it emitted a shock wave, and the head of the ogre went flying away and the ogre turned to dust.

For a second, I was so cocked up, that I thought that my head will explode! But then I managed to calm myself down, and, went towards the mysterious warrior.

"I am sorry for the interruption by these hunter ogres your highness," he said, "I had no idea that they will come even here for you!"

"But why so many monsters were trying to kill me?" I asked him.

"With all due respect my lady, I am not in the position to discuss this kind of matter with you in this dimension, but I give you my word, that after reaching Galdarth, I will clear all your questions"

He continued, "But for now, in this dimension, everything is at peace, for the time being."

The horseman came near me, sheathing his big double edged sword. He bow down, and then stood up, I said while staring at him, "So according to you, he is my guardian?"

"Yes your majesty," the warrior replied.

"So, does obeying my orders, include in his job?"

"I have no doubt that they won't"

"So he'll do whatever I tell him to?"

"Yes your majesty"

This made me smile, as I had names of many girls in class whose rolling heads on the ground won't make me sad, but when the warrior realized what I had in my mind, he immediately said, "Please your majesty, don't even bring any evil thought in your mind, the horseman will protect you, but he won't kill any person, who, according to him, cannot harm you"

"But, he still will obey my orders, right?"

"Yes"

And then just as he finished his word, I ordered, "I order the Headless horseman, to jump continuously" and the scene was mother of all hilariousness, the way my Guardian was jumping made me laugh my head off, when he was finished, then I ordered "Snap my guardian!" and then, he made such a fine tuning by his snapping fingers, that it occurred to me, what if I bring him to a party, and give him an official job of a 'snapper' and then I ordered him to do a 'cartwheel' he rolled and rolled till the mysterious warrior looked at me with such a way that was just like my chemistry teacher.

"Okay, just one last time" I assured him, and said, "Now, I order you to whistle!" but he didn't do anything, I repeated, yet he didn't do anything. I kept on repeating the order till the warrior told me "I am sorry for disturbing you, your majesty, but he can't whistle, you see, he has no head."

The same thought once again, made me shiver, but then, the warrior said "Oh great guardian, your work has been done, you may go" the horse man bowed down, and went riding away on his steed.

He took out a flask having a green colored liquid from his jacket pocket. He poured it on the hard ground, and within the matter of seconds, the liquid transformed into the glass slide! A big five foot tall five foot wide glass slide!

"So, shall we begin our journey?" he asked me,

"What do you want me to do?" I asked him "Jump on it?" on this remark; he gave me such a glance that was saying 'What else do you expect'. But before I could even realize what was going on, he grabbed my arm, we both jumped on the mirror, and everything went blank

Chapter 3

Mission Galdarth

This chapter will kick the butt of all the science teachers, so hang on...

For a second, I thought I was about to break my back, but nothing happened, when I opened my eyes then I saw that I am Drowning in a green colored water, But I was hardly wet! And I could breathe in the liquid, which occurred really strange to me!!!

"What the hell is happening?" I said to myself. Suddenly a voice said in my head, "We cannot waste any more time please follow me".

When I looked around then I saw that the warrior was beside me. Then, once again a voice told me in my head, "Worry not, we can read each others thought in this liquid, now, if you'll follow me." He swam through the water pointing at a window. There were two windows, one was from my world, and other was from his, something inside me was constantly urging me not to go with him, but I had made up my mind that I will go with him.

The warrior went out of the window first, and I followed him. When I came out, then we were on a beach of some kind, the weather was a little cold, and cool breeze was constantly blowing. Near the horizon, there were grasslands that resembled like the prairies, having only a dozen of trees in that whole area. I could also see mountain peaks far, far away, totally white, as if they were filled with ice.

"What was that mirror kind of thing?" I asked.

"I better close the entrance, the mirror, is the gateway to different dimensions, if not closed quickly after a portal leap, then it can destroy the reality and fabric of nature, the force applied by two dimensions will blast each other." The warrior said, he slammed his fist against the glass slide, and it broke to pieces, and then he buried the pieces in the sand.

"My god, the wind is so cool, yet the sun rays are so strong, better get under the shade of a tree before I get sunburns, damn these two suns" but suddenly, I repeated my sentence saying, "Did I just said, 'Two Suns?'"

As I looked up, I realized that there were in fact two suns! One was slightly bigger than the other, but there were two suns!

"Where are we?" I asked him, gazing at the two shining suns, which unlike our world's sun, did not hurt the eyes while looking at it.

The warrior cheerfully said "My Lady, I humbly welcome you, this is my birth place, and this is my Dimension, the planet of Galdarth."

"So what exactly is Galdarth?" I asked him. He started walking and advised me to follow him. My sneakers and my legs rubbed against the sandy ground beneath me.

"Just like your world, there are hundreds of different parallel earths, or worlds, and Galdarth is one of them, now without further ado, I must order you to follow me, time is less, and the Journey is long, we must make haste" he said and marched on. I followed him. We walked for almost fifteen minutes and then we left the beach area and entered the prairie area. I walked while trying to remove some of the small pebbles which entered in my sneakers.

"So where are you taking me?" I asked him.

"I am ordered to take you to a friend of mine, who is supposed to be waiting for us, and later when he joins us, then we both will escort you to our king" he answered back.

"Hey, um--- what's your name apart from being called the 'Mysterious warrior,' you promised me that you'll answer my questions when we reach Galdarth, now we have, so I want some answers, Like who are you, and what is drill" I asked him as I walked over the dry grass.

"My name is Lucius, and my Ranking in the knights is one of the elites, and about your answers my lady, all I can tell you that you have a very important role in our civilization, that is why we mark you as our queen. For the rest of your queries, I will keep my word, but at first, we must get to my friend, he must be waiting for us."

"So, who is your friend?" I asked him.

"You'll know soon enough" He replied

"Is he like you?"

"In a manner of speaking yes, but he is far more stronger than me, I am no match to his strength"

"Stronger than you! You could lift a passenger bus as if you were lifting a cricket bat; I sure want to meet that guy"

"You will meet him my lady, very soon"

"Ok, But I don't see anyone near! Where is your friend?"

"He is not near; he is waiting for us for about 12 Zilos away from here"

"Meaning?" this guy, really had no sense on how to talk to someone from another place, half of the time, I could not understand what he meant.

"He is over 60 to 65 kilometers away from our current position"

"What! Then how do you think we'll reach it before nightfall!" I exclaimed. I really was very confused about the drill. This guy really had a problem of speaking in riddles.

"By the help of them!" he said while pointing towards a tree that was almost 200 meters away. He was actually pointing to the horses that were tied from the trunk of the tree.

I gave a sigh of relief when I thought that I won't be needing to walk over 65 kilometers to meet a guy. But as I reached near, those horses seemed to be a little different, and then I realized that they may not be horses at all!

"Hey Lucius," I said, "You know what, though I was never into animals, and I never had much knowledge about them, but I can seriously argue that the Horses do not have horns! What are those?"

"I never said that we'll be using horses now, did I?" He replied, "We will use Unicorns, they are three times faster than any horse, and they are more calm"

"Unicorns! I am beginning to like this place!" I exclaimed.

"Yes I can see that," he said, "But you haven't seen anything yet".

"Now," he ordered, "the white one with pink horn is yours and the brown one with white horn is mine" he said when we reached the tree. Everything was going fine till now, but the only thing that I was sad about was that I didn't brought my camera, I could have made an image of myself if my schoolmates could see this.

Lucius patted his Unicorn and climbed on it, and asked me to do the same. But there was only a teeny-weeny-itsy-bitsy problem.

I never like horses; in fact I never liked animals, let alone unicorns. I knew tons of guys who got paralyzed or died due to this Riding-on-the-horse fever.

"Hey, Lucius, I think we have a major problem, how the hell can I get on this thing!" I exclaimed, and before the same second could pass, the Unicorn hit me by its hairy tail! "Could it understand what I just said?" I blurted out after watching it's reaction.

"She, is not an 'it'" Lucius replied rolling his eyes, "her name is Noel, like my unicorn's is Phillip, and if you want to get on her, then you can order, you are her master so she will understand what you say, just now you have seen that she understood what you said"

I was feeling really stupid but I had to get on the Unicorn, so I said in a weak voice, "Noel would you mind bending down a little, just a little, so that I can climb on you." The Unicorn looked at me with her big drooping eyes, and then rolled them as if saying 'Go to hell'.

Then I added, "Can you Bend down just a little, Please" and on my astonishment, she really bend down. 'Courtesy really helps in winning the heart, especially of a lady' I thought while getting on. I hooked up my backpack on the Unicorn's saddle hook, and then hoisted myself up.

"Now your Majesty, please follow me." He said while bowing down, and then rode off on his unicorn with great speed. I shouted "let's roll noel!" And then I tried to feel as if we were dashing, but in reality, my unicorn didn't move an inch! She was just eating the grass!

"Do you want me to tell you a special magic word?" I said while watching her eating the grass, she didn't even looked at me, her whole mind was just on eating the grass, and she was totally ignoring me!

"Ok, I'll try, Yee-Haw!! Noel!" I shouted but nothing happened, Lucius was so far that it was now hard to see him, he kept riding on. I had to make this mother of all ponies obey me, so I tried different versions of making a horse obey command. And I started shouting:

"Run!" Nothing happened.

"Start" Nothing happened.

"Accelerate!" Nothing happened.

"To infinity and beyond!" Nothing Happened!

"By the power of Gray-skull!" Nothing Happened

"TALLY HO!!" Nothing Happened!

"Oh for god sake will you just run noel PLEASE!" and before the second could even pass she galloped with such a speed that it was difficult for me to even balance my weight. 'So now I get it' I thought, 'she obeys my command on the word please!'

"Noel!" I commanded her, "Follow Lucius PLEASE!" and galloping at the top of her speed, my unicorn quickly caught up with Lucius. We rode on for a couple of hours, till we arrived at the beginning of a forest. Lucius got down from his Unicorn and helped me to do the same. I was about to fall just by looking at the size of the trees. They were taller than redwood easily, and were almost two to three feet wide. Their leaves were pink in color, and some of them were bearing fruits!

"Those are way too tall trees" I said in astonishment, "Even for a tree"

"Yes My queen" Lucius said "This is the beetle woods, and they are famous for such kinds of trees, their height can easily go up to 200 feet of your world."

"Two hundred feet!" I blurted out. This planet, or dimension was though very unknown, yet it was filled with the beauty of nature.

Far away (Not very far away), I could see an old castle on a hilltop; some of its towers were broken down. It was a kind of thing that we cannot see in now days. I was so curious to know everything about this planet, such as its nature, its animals, its inhabitants, even the planet itself!

Lucius went near a tree, and started waiting for something, or 'someone'. He was growing impatient by the minute, tapping his foot or muttering some words in a foreign language. It didn't took me long to understand that Lucius was one of those guys who get tensed up very easily. I sat down under the shade of a tree.

There was something that was very unusual about Lucius, since the time I met him, he didn't remove his helmet, and all I could see was his eyes. His eyes surely reminded me of someone, but I didn't know who.

I was busy in trying to remember something about his eyes when suddenly, I felt as if someone was watching us, though it was not like the feeling when I confronted the werewolf or the ogres, but it was a feeling which warned me that we are being watched. As if something was about to happen, something bad.

Suddenly I heard a low growl of a wolf, which made my goose bumps stand. I went to Lucius to warn him, and I said "I think that there is another Demon-Wolf nearby"

"That's impossible, the Demon-Wolves never leave their island, are you certain that you heard something," he answered

"Yes I am sure, and don't you say the word 'impossible' you sure do remember that a werewolf was just about to kill me in my world" I snapped.

"That was one of the elites my queen, and he was a bounty hunter, so he was not bound by the treaties"

"Are you sure, because I seriously doubt it" I replied, but he didn't reply. Just to make myself sure that no one was near us, I tried to investigate it on my own.

While the elite knight was busy in waiting for someone, he didn't even realize that I was gone (just a few yards away). Though I was suspicious, I couldn't find anything. Just when I was about to go back, a bush behind me rustled.

And just as I went near it, I saw 2 big green eyes, and a growl of a wolf. Just as I took a step back, a giant animal pounced on me. I fall down, and when I opened my eyes then I saw that the animal was actually a huge wolf! It was over thrice the size of any horse (or unicorn for instance)

He was having claws so big that it will make even a lion feel like a domestic house cat. His teeth were bigger than a chef's knife, his fur was grey color, and his eyes were green, hungry angry green.

His big jaws were just a couple of centimeters away from my face, sniffing me and growling at me. In mad desperation I shouted "LUCIUS, HELP!" and thank god he saw me. He dashed towards me, though he was just twenty to thirty meters away, it felt as if he is coming from over a mile away.

The big wolf sniffed me for one last time, and I thought 'this is the end, oh my god, I forgot to tell my parents that Where I hid my diary, well, thank god, I still don't want them to know my secrets.' (Now I don't know if I was happy or sad ok).

He was sniffing me as if sniffing dead meat, and after sniffing me for one last time, all of a sudden, his whole behavior changed! He sat down and did the worst imaginable thing; he licked me with his big 1 foot long tongue!

"Yuck" was the only word that came out of my mouth. He started barking happily like a dog, and just as Lucius reached, he started laughing like a child! He laughed and laughed till his stomach hurt and tears came out of his eyes.

"Why the hell are you laughing?" I exclaimed, the big wolf, on watching Lucius, ran towards him and started licking him happily. Both of them were acting as if they were some owner pet relationship between them.

Lucius tried to stop the wolf, by saying "Stop boy, stop it, it tickles, stop it Fang, stop!"

"You have named your wolf!" I asked him surprisingly, "Oh my god, now what, I am really scared of dogs, I should have told you before, I hate dog, I have *DOGOPHOBIA!" (No I just made up this word)*

"He is not a dog, he is a wolf, pet wolf, but we are good friends, his name is Fang, say hello to the queen Fang" Lucius said while addressing me as the queen.

"You have a four meter tall grey wolf as your pet!!" I exclaimed while swatting away the entire wolf's saliva from my face.

"He is not my pet; he is my friend's pet! It is a category my queen, he is the supreme wolf; known for his loyalty, and on him rides the supreme knight, who is my friend, with whom you will just be meeting." he replied.

"Oh, where is your so called friend!" I shot back, I must admit, I wasn't happy, and who will be, after being licked to jelly by a giant hound!

Lucius took out a small-portable-telescope kind of thingy (which was soooooo 18th century), looked through it and pointed on the old hill fort and said "There is my friend" he said. I gazed there, took the telescope and saw through it. I could see a figure of a man, or possibly a boy. The image was quite far away almost hundreds of meters away.

The figure was on the topmost tower of the fort, and was probably looking at us. Just as when I thought that what will happen, the figure, ran toward the edge of the tower, and jumped so high that it was hard for me to see him.

"Who is that guy?" I asked Lucius, trying to figure out where the guy has gone, up in the clouds, "surely enough he can't be the one you said to be your friend, is he Lucius?"

"He is the one your majesty, the supreme knight" Lucius said while tugging my hand, "and now, will you care to take a few steps back, my friend loves to make a dramatic entry". I took a few steps back, watching as the guy came falling down from the sky.

"I think a little more far will do" Lucius instructed me. Just as I took a few steps back (Again) the falling guy landed just a few meters away from my spot. He landed on feet, and his landing was so strong that it emitted a shock wave and the spot where he landed, the ground broke.

I went near him with Lucius and with Fang (The giant wolf). The guy was a knight too no doubt, but his helmet was of red color, unlike Lucius's one which was of white color. His dragon slayer logo was also of red color, while Lucius's one was of white color but everything else was same, he was wearing leather-biker jacket, with black jeans, black belt and black pointy old man shoes.

"Your Majesty" Lucius said "I introduce you, Sir Marcus, one of the last of The Supreme Knights of Galdarth."

The supreme knight bowed down and said "Pleased to meet you your majesty, it is one of the most honorable movements of my life." His tone was very regal but was way too familiar. Just like Lucius.

"The honor is mine- I guess" I said weakly trying to make them feel as if they are talking to someone having a royal status.

"Lucius," said Marcus to the Elite knight, "are you certain that she is the 'one'?"

"Yes Marcus, I cannot be wrong, even Fang has made his statement that she is the only 'one', so there is no doubt that she is the 'one'" Lucius replied.

"Enough of the 'one', I am still confused what is going on, and who are you guys?" I shot back at them, but it didn't matter as both of them were busy in their own talks.

"Yes I think that now is the time, where we tell her our true identity" Marcus instructed. "I had the same thought bearing in my mind too!" Lucius added. Upon their word, both of them closed their eyes, and started concentrating.

Suddenly, their helmet started transforming! The front part of the helmet was reduced, the upper part and the side part reduced, and right next second, it changed into goggles, having the same shape of their eye area of helmet.

And I was so shocked to see the faces of those two guys, which the transforming of the helmet part seemed like nothing!

Marcus and Lucius were none other than my classmates Madhav and Amrit!

I felt as I am being choked to death, the werewolf incident or the ogre incident, heck, even the parallel world theory was not as crazy as watching two of my friends become so strong!

I was so angry by this surprise, that without wasting another second, I ran towards Lucius, and slammed him on the ground! I couldn't think that I was actually fighting with someone who was maybe ten thousand times stronger than me!

"Why didn't you tell me who you are?" I said wrapping my hands around his neck and squeezing it, "WHY DIDN'T YOU TELL ME!" the big wolf started barking at me, may be telling to stop this, but for that time, nothing seemed to bother me!

"For I knew—" he gagged, "That this would—be-your re—reaction!" Marcus came to help Lucius, but I didn't let him!

"EXPLAIN!" I shouted, and Lucius shot back "by the time I'd explain it to you, YOU'D BE DEAD!!" his voice was so strong that it reminded me, about the werewolf incident, that he saved my life for a couple of times! And this behavior could not help any of us. So I left Lucius, and he started breathing like he was having asthma!

"Oh by a Knight's beard," he said catching his breath, "She is more difficult to handle than any other monster!" and then he added, "Oh I am sorry my queen, I seemed to have lost a bit of temper"

"No, it was my fault" I replied calmly "I shouldn't have made it such an issue, I am sorry, but who are you guys anyway?"

"We" replied Marcus "May confuse you to be your friends, but actually we are their parallel beings, remember my queen, that we are in fact from a parallel dimension"

"That means you are not Madhav," I said pointing at Marcus, "And that you're not Amrit!" I said pointing at Lucius.

"No we are not." Marcus said, "But you are wise to be confused. They are but a reflection of our lives in your world. Our life in your planet is in a human form and in your world we are your classmates. But here, we two are warriors. We are assigned to escort you to our king Sir Nortus, and from there on, you shall take the throne of Galdarth!"

"But, why only me?"

"I could tell it to you now, but I must not, for the trees here have ears" he said gazing at the forest.

After calming myself down, Marcus and Lucius made the preparations for our journey, and took out some old maps, and studied them carefully, I tried to look at it, and to understand it, but it was written in some another language. There were at least four to five maps.

After studying them carefully, we all packed our sacks, (I packed my 'Bag', and there is a difference.) And we were ready. Lucius showed me the map and said, "My queen, at first we pass through the beetle woods, that you see in the front, and then from there we'll cross the sander lands north. After that we'll arrive at Derekus Hills. After crossing the mountain ranges, we'll reach at Ginger woods. Soon we'll be greeted by a town, known as Draston, then we'll take a boat to cross the primus sea, and after that, from one day march, we'll reach at Kingslograd, home of the Knights. According to me, our journey will end in over five to six days."

"So I think that we should move right now" I said, as I climbed on Noel, my pet Unicorn.

"That's the Spirit!" Lucius said cheerfully.

And we marched on. At first I knew something awesome was going to happen in this journey, but I had no idea that my expectations would prove to be quite small.

Chapter 4

Nikita V.s. an ORC!

For half of the day, we were trotting on the back of our animals, and during that time, all I could see were trees, with pink leaves, trees with pink leaves, trees with pink leaves. We all were trying to find a place to sleep for that day, as the ground was either covered in wet mud, or with bushes and shrubs.

Though the scenic beauty was breathtaking, but everything has a limit for god's sake, and I was being way too bored, so to pass time, I took out my Mp3 and started listening to its music.

And just in other coming five minutes, Marcus, unable to stop his curiosity, came and asked, "What Kind of strange contraption is this?" I realized that he had never seen an Mp3 player before, so just to see his reaction, I gave it to him.

"This" I said taking out my earplugs, "this is an Mp3 player, and it plays music that you have stored in it"

"It is quite peculiar to see that a musician can fit inside such a tiny thing" he replied while studying the player. I turned it on, and he widened his eyes, "most extraordinary, what kind of strange magic does this thing uses?"

"Uh, not magic but, battery, it runs on a battery" I replied

"What is a battery?" he asked me again, his questions were never ending, which reminded me of Madhav, but telling someone such kind of questions, seemed very awkward to me, so, I said, "Stop asking questions, put on the earplugs and enjoy the music."

"Can it play Galdarthian folk song?"

"Just put it on now, will you?"

He did so, and suddenly his whole body started shivering! As if the tunes were being filled up in his head. "It is very amazing" he replied, "I don't know why, but I feel like I have to dance now, not with a partner like a classical song, but, solo!" he replied, which was typical as he was listening to an exotic song by my favorite band.

He started humming while listening, and his faithful wolf, Fang, after looking at his master, shook his head in disgrace which made me laugh. The big wolf was smarter than any other animal I had ever seen, in fact, all the animals, like our unicorns, and the wolf, were giving out human emotions that I could understand.

At that point I thought that though Marcus and Madhav were dimensions apart, they had many things in common, both of them were very smart, very Naive and adorable. Apart from Marcus's regal nature and strong physique, he had a lot of things in common with Madhav.

Soon, we reached at a place that was not totally covered shrubs, or soaked mud, it was almost as wide as the basket ball arena. Marcus ordered everyone to halt, and giving me my Mp3 back, and thanking me, he said "Lucius, we shall spend the night here my friend, I will collect fire wood, while you can get some food" he went away and disappeared in the forest on his fang

"I will be happy to help" Lucius replied, which really got me thinking, that as they were from the medieval period, so they can kill an animal for food, but the problem was, that I was a total vegetarian, so there was no chance that I could eat meat.

"Uh for the food Lucius, can I take your five minutes?" I asked him.

"Yes my queen, what shall you need?"

"There is a problem, I am a vegetarian, meaning that I can't eat meat, so, do you have any bright ideas so that I do not starve to death?" I asked. I was so upside down because of my running emotions that I forgot I had packed enough food to last for a week!

"Worry not your highness" he replied, "Beings in this dimension do not eat meat" he replied. As he unloaded a cotton sack from the bag of his unicorn. This was not as I expected I thought that they will roast a pig or any other animal and then gulp it down, "so you mean you guys are vegetarian?"

"No, I mean all of Galdarthian humans are vegetarians" he replied while knotting his unicorn and mine. "In the ancient laws, written by the demon wizard Zorodast the Great, it is said that, those who eat Animals, in our dimension, shall not be considered as humans, for killing someone for food, while having other things to eat, is considered a sin, at least in our World."

"Then what are we going to eat?" I asked him, feeling happy that we will not kill a poor animal, while also being confused about what we will be eating.

"Would you like to see my lady? You then follow me" he said with a happy smile on his face. On finding nothing interesting to do, I voted to go with him. The sky was getting orange, and I had no intention of staying alone if it got dark.

So I walked with him, and on every minute, I tried to dodge muddy water on the ground, I could not afford to get my sneakers dirty. We were walking for at least twenty minutes, and then just as when I was going to quit, Lucius said pointing at some of the mushrooms, "Look down my lady, this is what we will eat."

I had to confess that I never liked mushrooms, and since childhood, I was a very fussy eater. But I knew that here, I had to make an exception. He collected almost a dozen of such kinds of mushrooms, and stuffed it in his sack.

"Now for the fruits" he said, he took out his goggles, wore it and concentrated. In no time his goggles transformed back to his white colored helmet. He went near a tall tree, held it and started shoving it gently, as if shoving a very delicate thing.

Before I could understand what he was doing, an apple fell right on my head. And from then on, almost a dozens of fruits started falling down. The thing which astonished me was that even though, Lucius was shoving only a particular tree, at least three different kinds of fruits were falling down like apple mango orange, even grapes!

"Here in Galdarth, one tree can bear at least three fruits" Lucius said after watching my astonishment. His helmet transformed back to his goggles, and he put them in his Jacket pocket, "Now, shall we take a stroll to fetch some water?" he said.

He took me to a nearby stream, took out his bottle and started filling it up. Everything was so peaceful, the birds were chirping, and the trees were bristling. The air was fully re-energizing. This was a place where anyone would like to live for the rest of his life.

"All right" Lucius said as he closed the bottle cap, "Let's get back to our camp, Marcus must be waiting for us and............" suddenly his voice trailed off. I tried to see why he started acting so strange, but I could not understand what it was. He started looking everywhere, as if he had seen a ghost.

"Cut to the chase Lucius and tell me what's going on?" I asked him becoming irritated. He held his finger on his lips signing me to stop talking. "Can you hear it my lady?" he asked.

"Can I hear what?"

"The silence, hear the silence, something is wrong, the trees are not supposed to act like this."

"Lucius, now you're freaking me out."

"The trees are trying to warn us" he said, and all of a sudden, he dropped his bottle, and started running. I tried to follow him but he was too fast. Somehow I managed to catch up with him, but when I looked at him then I saw his eyes, full of dread.

When I saw what had happened then I had to avert my eyes, there was a big corpse of a boar, bigger than a SUV car. From his back, a large chunk of meat was torn down.

"The facial expressions of the boar can tell us that it was not done by an animal. Look at his wounds, no animal in Galdarth is so ferocious; this poor animal was eaten alive." Lucius said, "This is not done by an animal, the wound is not more than five hours old, and the bite size and massive jaws power leads me to only one possible solution, that we are not alone in the forest, someone is watching, some is here to hunt us down, and that someone is a vicious monster"

"How can you say that it is not done by an animal, I think that a giant wolf like Fang, can easily bring such kind of animal down." I argued. At that point, I myself was so scared that just to make myself feel secure; I tried to contradict Lucius's judgment.

"If it was killed by another animal, then it should have been transformed in to statue and then to dust right after the attacker would have its fill. And any animal does not attack on the back; they usually target the throat for an instant kill. But as you can see it is not, so I do think that this is what the trees were warning us about. I reckon that we should head back to the camp right now my lady" he said. We both wandered back to our camp, and I gave one last glimpse to the poor animal, he was looking so scared and so, dead.

Back in the camp Lucius started cooking the mushroom soup on the fireplace. It was very funny watching a great warrior in an apron humming while cooking. He was a very adorable at that point. And somehow I seemed to forget that in front of me was person standing strong enough to toss away big buses like a ragdoll.

I stood up and looked up at the sky, the moon in this place was much bigger than we had on our earth, and it was almost three times bigger. I sat on the ground watching the beauty of nature, and listening to the sweet sound of the night life of the forest, when I was suddenly interrupted by Marcus.

"Lucius told me about your today's encounter your highness" he said calmly, "but I give you my word, no harm shall come to you on my watch. You can count on me"

I knew that he was true to his word, but something was wrong and I knew it especially after watching the big boar being torn, so I replied "I do trust you Marcus, but I also know the hard truth, which is that I am so weak that I can hardly protect myself from anything, such as a monster, a demon, or whoever wants me dead."

Suddenly Marcus's face lighten up, and with his cheerful disposition, he stood up and ran towards Fang. He took out a thing or two from his sack, which at that time was not very visible to my eyes due to the darkness.

But as he came near, my happiness knew no bounds! I soon realized that he was bringing two awesome things for me. He was bringing silver visor-specs, and a white leather jacket. I was trying to hide my happy expressions, as I guessed that those two things were for me!

"My lady," he said, "these are for you". I actually snatched both of them away from Marcus. He was very surprised to see this kind of behavior from what he called 'his queen' (WHAT? You guys know I had that coming!)

"How do you wear this?" I asked putting on the specs. But, before Marcus could even answer, I started feeling as if the specs were transforming, transforming and covering my whole face. For the first couple of minutes, everything was dark. I could not see a thing. Then later Marcus's face became visible, and soon, the hazy background became clearer.

"I am sorry for the inconvenience my lady" Marcus said "but when a person wears his helmet for the first time. Then it takes some moments to initialize, but don't worry, next time it will take place in a split second."

To be true, I was not even listening to him, I was astonished to see the world through the helmet. I could zoom over hundreds of meters away, I could see the number of trees by a special eco vision, and I could see Marcus's internal bones, his organs and even his beating heart! And all this just by a little concentrating!!!!

"So do you like it your majesty? This helmet which you are wearing is called lunar ray, it was made by the light of the Galdarthian moon by our first knight ever, the Zarthur. And this was one of his first helmets that he wore." Marcus asked me.

"Are you kidding, who won't like this piece of work in this whole universe?" I replied still amazed to see the world through the helmet. Not only it was making me watch things which were beyond the reach of physical or mental potential but was explaining it too. Just by a little amount of concentration.

I could read about the nature and wildlife of the planet which was coming on the eye-screen. IT WAS AWESOME!!!

As I looked at Marcus the eye-screen started typing like this:

NAME: SIR MARCUS

OCCUPATION: KNIGHT

RANK: SUPREME KNIGHT

ABILITIES: ULTIMATE STRENGTH, GENIUS LEVEL INTELLECT, BORN TO BE A GREAT LEADER, EXTREMELY LOYAL, EXPERIENCE OF OVER THIRTEEN HUNDRED BATTLES WITHOUT ANY DEFEATS.

SUPREME COMMANDER OF THE CENTURION BATTALION AND SECOND STRONGEST KNIGHT AFTER NORTUS.

RECORD: WINNING OVER THIRTEEN HUNDRED BATTLES AGAINST THE VANDALS, NEVER COMITTING A SIN, RECORD OF NOT KILLING EVEN A SINGLE ENEMY EVEN AFTER DEFEATING HIM. DEFEATED AN ENTIRE ARMADA ALONE

DEFEATS: NONE

"I am reading about you Marcus" I said slyly.

"Oh you wish to see my victories your majesty, well, I do not like to boast but well you know, people do call me what they say in your world AWESOME" he replied, "well enough research for one night, now it is time for you to test your strength my queen"

This was what I was waiting for; I could not wait to see how strong I could be. Marcus took me a little further deep in the forest, and then stopped in front of a big thick tree. It was almost a couple of foot wide, had a very thick and strong bark, which felt like sandpaper, and looked very old and tough.

"You see my lady" Marcus began, "a knight's helmet, is a knight's power source, without his helmet, a knight is powerless, and can be killed like a mortal being, but with his helmet, a knight gets extraordinary superhuman strength. One thing that you should know is that the helmet, which any knight has, will only give power to the specific person, and not another person who manages to take the possession of the latter's helmet, in other words, your helmet chooses you instead of you choosing him, which means that your helmet will obey only your command and no one else's, and as an addition, a knight's helmet also helps him to breath in the vacuum of space, or breath underwater without any time limit."

"There are three kinds of knights your majesty, the first one, or the basic one is the ranger knight, which possesses the blue helmet, it is a basic helmet which enhances the power, speed and agility of any person drastically. Then comes an elite knight, such as Lucius. An elite knight posses a white helmet, and possesses power far greater than any ranger knight, you saw it very well when he lifted a big bus as if it weighed almost nothing.

This stuff was so cool that I could not even think of anything else apart from thinking about their power, that's why Lucius could lift a whole 22 ton bus as if he was lifting a softball. But then it occurred to me, what about Marcus's power, or the power of the supreme knight, Marcus was telling me how one becomes a knight, but I was not listening to him anymore, I concentrated and tried to compare a supreme knight's power with that of a ranger knight, and the answer was way too cool, my helmet indicated that power of a supreme knight can reach to over infinity, depending upon to pureness of one's heart, a supreme knight was strong enough to do almost anything, ANYTHING!!!!

Suddenly Marcus snapped his fingers in front of me and continued, "so as I was saying, a knight defense comes from his jacket, this jacket is strong enough to withstand from the heat of a star till the freezing temperatures of the of the outer space, it also protects from the enemies blows, but, a ranger knight jacket, can only take blows from another ranger knight as an elite knight can take from another elite knights or a supreme knight can take on another supreme knight. If a knight fights someone beyond his rank, then his death is imminent."

"So how does a ranger knight kill another ranger knight?" I asked.

"Good question my queen" Marcus said, "just like a human, ranger knights power is multiplied, with respect to his original strength, so power vary even in ranger knights"

"Now time for your field test my lady. Try to break this tree with one punch" he said pointing out at the tough old tree.

Though I was very excited, I was very scared too, I was not sure whether I will break the tree or my bones because no one ever asked me to do these kinds of things ever before in my life.

"You're kidding right, I don't think that I can break it" I replied hesitatingly.

"We don't know it for sure right?" he replied

"But what if I break my hand?"

"No, you won't, I promise you, now shall we?"

"I am not sure"

"WILL YOU JUST PUNCH IT?"

Marcus forced me so hard that I had no other choice. I concentrated my energy into my fist, and gave the tree a strong left hook. For a few milliseconds, I was trying to make myself ready for the pain that was about to spurge in me, but just as I punched the tree, my fist broke a large chunk of wood from the tree, and within seconds, the tree fell down.

Within seconds I realized how big the tree was. It was easily over 5 foot wide, and had a bark of over half a foot thick, and the tree was over 150 feet tall. And it came crashing down with a huge thud. The fall was so strong that it shook the whole area, and lots of birds flew away from the danger.

"OH my god!!!" I shouted in excitement, "Did you see that, I just broke the tree, this was so easy, and I didn't even use half of my strength!!"

"Yes, my queen," replied Marcus, "that is what I was telling you, with these weapons, you have got the----" suddenly he was interrupted by someone.

"Hey what in the name of gods great beard are you two doing?" the person was none other than Lucius, he was wearing an apron, and a chef hat, he was also carrying a big bowl with a big wooden spoon and mixing something in it.

Marcus then added "But I should advise you not to challenge any elite knight for a duel, you have seen Lucius's power a while back on earth, well to be true he didn't even use 20% of his strength."

"Come on you two, the dinner is almost ready" he said. We all went back to our camp, "I have made an excellent mushroom soup for you both," he gave me a big bowl, and said, "First you try it my queen" when I saw the soup, then it made me lose my appetite, it was a grey colored thick liquid, thicker than any other soup.

But when I thought about refusing to have it, two options of the coming event stopped me:

A: after watching the excited face of Lucius made me feel bad on my part,

B: I could not afford to make Lucius angry or sad because he could hit me so hard that I could fly out in outer space by the force.

Gathering courage, I took a spoon, and tasted the thick soup, I was ready to spit it out, but I realized that it was far more delicious than I had in many years. I drank 2 more bowls, and suddenly I remembered that I had packed my food two, so I said "as Lucius you gave me your recipe, I will give you mine," I took out one lunchbox, and handed it to them both.

"What are these, my lady?" Marcus asked

"It is called a sandwich" I replied, and now I think I shouldn't have said that.

"SAND-WHITCHES, WHERE ARE THEY?" Marcus shouted, and immediately Lucius took on his helmet, and crushed the sandwiches so hard that it tremor the whole area!

"Guys!" I said rolling my eyes "sandwich, not sandwitch, they're good, try it." I gave another one to them, at first, they were cautious, them after studying it from there mask, they agreed to eat it. As they took a bite, I could see that those two didn't like it, it was hard for them to swallow it down, but somehow they managed to do so.

And after this, they even had the guts to say this! Marcus said catching his breath "these were—very---very delicious my queen, but we are full, we shall eat no more, but yes, you are—you are a very good cook"

And I replied sarcastically "and you both are very good actors". After a while, Lucius and Marcus laid down our beds and I started taking out my night-suit from my bag.

"Hey, Marcus," I asked for him "I have to change my clothes, so I will be needing you guys to go away from here"

"I do not think that it will be a wise decision my queen," he replied, "why not you sleep with the clothes you're wearing, and it will save our time tomorrow morning as well"

"But, you have to understand, I can't sleep in these!" I said pointing out my trekking clothes but then it hit me, "hey, I think the better idea will be that I should go away from the camp site, while you guys are busy doing the bed, I can very well change my clothes." Marcus looked defeated, he never thought that I was this persistent but eventually he agreed, and said "don't go too far!"

"What do you mean don't go too far, I have to be sure" I shot back as I started walking with my clothes.

"I mean that much far is good enough" he replied "we can make sure no harm is done to you as we have to keep watch, you should know that this forest is lurking with monsters"

"Have you lost your mind, I cannot let you watch me while I AM CHANGING!!" I shot back, though Marcus had no ulterior motives I couldn't let anyone see me.

"Ok at least stay in sight"

"ARE YOU CRAZY!!?"

Finally Marcus came to a conclusion that I should take my arsenal (Knight Helmet, and armor jacket) with me, for which I agreed too. I went inside the forest, and walked for another five minutes, when I was confirmed that no one was watching, I started changing.

I was almost finished when someone said in a very deep voice; "You should know not to change your clothes in public" I was totally freaked out. I had no idea in frigging hell who said that. Then suddenly the same voice said, "If you are looking for the one who said this, then I should advise you to look for 'something' rather than 'someone'"

I was not getting any meaning out of the sentence, but then, I saw someone moving behind a nearby tree, it was night sky so I could not see clearly but as I went near it took me some time to realize that no one was moving near the tree, the tree was the one which was moving by tilting from one point to another very slowly, I felt like face-palming myself, it was a TREE!! A talking tree. Slowly and slowly green eyes started coming out, then a huge beard made out of bark of the tree. This tree was not very tall, at most he could reach 30 feet, but still he was special because he could talk. I had seen many small trees in this forest but only this one could talk.

"I am ENT from the beetle woods, identify yourself or be-gone" he said slowly in a very booming voice, "what be your name young lady?"

"I am Nikita, Nikita Mehra, from—" I said but before I could complete the tree said "from earth?" for which I nodded, then he added "accompanied by great warriors? Both are knights? One elite and other the supreme?" I nodded again.

"Oh sweet trees, bring me the joy from the holy god of beetle-woods" he said happily and continued, "Then the prophecy is true!"

"Which prophecy?" I asked, I could not afford to lose this conversation, it would mean the answers to all of my queries. "You have to tell me everything" I cried.

"Like 'everything' everything?" he replied again slowly.

"Yes for starters what is it, think of me as a tourist, and now guide me" I said.

"What is a tourist" he said. He was literally pissing me off.

"Stop asking so many questions, give me facts, details, history, prophecy, reasons, I want to know everything" I cried angrily.

"Are you certain that the knowledge which I am about to share with you will not, now how do I say it, blast your brain, because no one from your world can comprehend this, you have to be the chosen one" he warned,

"Grandpa, will you just spill the beans please" I growled.

"Well, seems to me that you are a persistent one, aren't you" he said.

"Can we get on with it?" I said face-palming myself.

"Ok so let us begin" he replied "but let me ask you, what do you think about mythology, what is it for you?"

"History, or ancient history I guess" I answered.

"well, yes and no, you see in the era of Globalization, when man was at the peak of his curiosity, he started conquering the regions from his own planets, he started killing his own kinds, so the gods, who were watching, knew that they could not do anything, the force of man was beyond their control now, and as the new man arrived, the older version who believed in gods started fading away, the earth was now ruled by humans, and was bathing in their bloodshed now. This much bloodshed made gods very angry, they had only two options, either to kill all the life on earth or start again, or leave the dimension."

"So gods from each mythology, such as Hindu gods from Hindu mythology, Greek Gods from their own mythology, Egyptian gods, Roman Gods, Aztec Gods, Inca gods, they all joined together and made separate dimension for each mythology such as a dimension known as INDRALOK or OLYMPUS or EGYPTIAN HEAVEN where now all the gods from their respected mythology lived"

"Gods started making new planets such as Galdarth in this dimension and Gladiatorinork in another and Sparticara, and like that at least hundreds more, and filled each of them with people. Man in these dimensions were better and more qualified in almost everything than man on earth. But then the men had nothing to do, still life went on and the gods made the limitations of men, most of the men in these dimensions are not more than farmers, small doctors, warriors, craftsman librarians, teachers, and to rule them, there would be a king. It is just like the history from earth, just men here are more enlightened."

"But then came the era of darkness" his tone became deeper, "the monsters from earth also wanted to make the truce from the gods, they wanted their separate dimensions to live, so gods gave them their wish and sent them to different dimensions, but they were a bit careless, they didn't send the monsters in their specific dimensions, and the monsters started rampaging on whichever planet they were on in order to rule it, when things went out of hands, then to stop this, gods made a force of people who would protect their dimension from the monsters, such as Knights of Galdarth, Spartans of Sparticara, Legionnaires and Gladiators of Gladiatorinork, and so on. And thus the long battle had begun."

"Ok" I said "I almost got everything but you still didn't answer my real question that what has it got to do with me and the destruction of earth?"

"But then I answered your question, which was telling you the history and facts about different dimensions." He replied, "well nevertheless, I shall answer your this query as well, you see, each dimension has its own prime ruler, which governs almost everything about the planet, the politics, the force, the people and even the nature itself. They are known as the 'Peacemakers' their presence makes the core of our planet stable, while in their absence, the planet is doomed to die."

"Though they are immortal, but this doesn't mean that they can't be killed, our Peacemaker, sacrificed her life for the greater good, but she started a chain of reaction which would actually mean the destruction of our planet, and as earth is the dimension nearest to ours, it will be destroyed too by supernova caused by your sun as the result of the fate of Galdarth, but this doesn't stops there, as earth is the master planet and is linked to all the other planets, they will die within a day after the destruction of earth. You Nikita Mehra are the direct re-incarceration of our peace queen, and so your presence on your throne will mean avoiding the fate of all the dimensions."

"Ok I am pretty sure that you have mistaken me for someone, I mean I seriously can't be what you're thinking. I can't manage my own life, how am I supposed to manage an entire planet?"

"You are the one for instance, you like to help others even though they cannot understand your behavior and your perception, those cannot understand you because you are different than people from that dimension, it is because you were never meant to be living on earth, your true home is on Galdarth, then again, You can't pay attention on a thing for too long, your mind is wandering, it is because your brain is made for ruling an entire planet which means many subjects at one time. Believe these words my queen and trust your friends, both will be of great help when the time needs them to be" He answered back.

This was way over my capacity to handle things, I mean, if I hadn't seen the werewolf or any other monster in real life in the first place; this stuff would've really blasted off my brain! Somehow I managed to slow down my breathing, and managed to remain calm.

Suddenly the Ent said, "My queen, we are not alone here, someone is watching us!"

I thought that it must be one of the knights, "Hey Lucius, is that you?"

"No my queen" Ent said, he was very terrified "This is not a knight, something else, of great evil, yes, I can see him" he started concentrating "he is coming for you my queen, run, RUN NOW, if he gets you, the worlds will end, you must run!!! And don't look back, go straight at your camp, and stay with the knights, they know how to protect you, go, And GO NOW!!!"

I took all the clothes that I could, and started running through the forest, though I could see nothing for a couple of minutes, I realized my grave mistake only when I stopped to catch my breath, "I've forgotten the way back to the CAMP!!" I shouted, this was a huge mess up, and that's all because of me. I started looking for a place where there is light, because Marcus instructed us not to put out the light, it will keep the animals away (which seemed pretty useless as he could kill an entire species without breaking a sweat)

I tried to find the fireplace but I still couldn't, the night was high and it was really creepy, and cold. 'I have to do something to protect myself from the cold winds, or I'll get sick!' I thought, and then it hit me, I could use the knight jacket to protect myself and the helmet to locate Marcus and Lucius. I did that the right next second, as I put on the helmet, I concentrated, and then through the X-ray vision, I located the camp, and both of the knights were sleeping in their bags, 'So much for protecting the queen' I thought to myself.

Just as I started walking at towards the campfire, someone slammed a hug tree right on my face!! The impact was so strong that I flew breaking at least a 5 trees on the way, thanks to the knight arsenal that I was not dead, though the impact nearly got me passed out. As I managed to open my eyes, I saw that there was a human-ish kind of figure, it was very muscular, and was at least 20 foot tall. As I saw it's faced I felt a shiver running from the back of my spine. It was a monster, it was of grey color, was wearing iron claps on each hand, and it was having spikes, it was wearing a underwear of Tarzan, its face was very disgusting, big face with no hair, small mouth and a very big nose, his teeth were in a very bad shape, he had a small horn coming out of his of his forehead, and he was way too big, he was just like the Ogres who attacked me, just only five to six times bigger. The Intel which my helmet gave me was like this:

SPECIES: ORC

RANK: BOUNTY HUNTER

EMPLOYER: UNKNOWN

ABILITIES: SUPERSTRENGTH, HEIGHT AS AN ADVANTAGE, GREAT DEFENCE WITH HANDS.

WEAKNESS: LACK OF A BRAIN MAKES HIM PREDICTABLE.

This stuff won't help me in the least, I never fought with anyone, heck I never watched any fighting shows, I hardly knew any move, I wasn't sure whether I'll survive the night or not. I was alert, watching the Orc's every move but before I could come up with a plan, he kicked me right on the chest!! Somehow I managed to brace for the impact, but this time also, I felt very less if compared to the actual force of the Orc.

The Orc kept staring at me, and started circling around me, so that he could find a weak spot, but I was sure not to give him any, this time when he ran towards me I was ready for him, as he came near to slam my little body with his big foot, I dodged it and jumped, I thought that I'll jump as high as I could, but what followed next was very awkward, I had such power that I jumped over 40 feet high in the air!

My landing was more than perfect, I landed right on the Orc's face, as we both fell, he groaned in pain. I tried to gain back my balance but I was having no idea what was coming for me. Then he started punching me rapidly, I could feel each punch, I could feel the energy, I could feel the pain, but it was like another human punching me with an average strength. I blocked one last punch of the Orc, and taking down the opportunity, punched him back on his chest,

I contracted all the power I could for the specific moment and then I punched him.

The force exerted was so strong that the Orc went flying away breaking a couple of tree in his way, he nearly passed out, but then, somehow got on his feat, and gained back consciousness and growled back at me. But now I wasn't afraid of him, I learnt how to tackle a giant monster and now I was ready (this time I mean really 'READY' ready)

He ran towards me, and started punching me on the face, but I started dodging his strong punches, and then, again as I saw the opportunity, I blocked his fist, and grabbed it with all my strength. The Orc started pushing me with his fist, and though my feet were stuck on the ground, he still could do this. But before he could slam me on a tree, I tilted a little and the Orc got slam head first on the tree's bark.

I got a little over confident in myself, and tried to end the fight my trying to slam my knee against the lying Orc's face. But I made a big mistake. As I aimed and jumped to hit his head, out of all the sudden, the Orc returned with a strong backhand which landed on my tiny body.

As I flew away breaking another tree, my visor showed that the distance between me and my camp was increasing drastically. The Orc was deliberately trying to get me away from the knights. I really needed to finish this.

As I regained my balance, I saw that the Orc was just about to grab me. But without wasting another

Second, I grabbed his arm, and gave him a very tight slam.

Then again he got on his feat, and again I started beating him, I started landing my strong punches on his body, he could barely withstand them! Finally when he was all tired and near to death, I tried to pass him out, as he was lying on the forest floor half dead, I jumped with all my strength and reached at least 90 feet in the air and landed right on his belly.

The Orc squealed in pain, and just as when I thought to hit him again, right next second he started to change, his face was calm, and he slowly started turning into stone.

"No, oh god what have I done?" I said to myself as my helmet transformed back to goggles. I never wanted to kill anyone, I just wanted to protect myself but I went too far.

"MARCUS! LUCIUS!!, HELP" I called out their names and tried to stop the transformation, but it was too late, and finally the Orc looked at me as if saying "Good luck for the rest of the journey" and died.

I started crying because it was the first time I killed someone, I went too far, I couldn't manage my powers, I was so sad on my part. I knew that the Orc would have done the same for me, but this wasn't what I wanted. The area was calm, and I couldn't hear anything apart from my own sad voice.

Then suddenly, I heard rustling behind the bushes, as if someone was coming, and whatever that was, it was coming fast, and I did not know what to do. "Back off" I shouted, "I know How to kill, I just killed an Orc, don't make me do that to you too.

And before I even got a chance to wear my helmet, Marcus came out from the bushes. He was not wearing his helmet, but had his jacket armor. He first saw me, and looked very happy. And then, when he saw a statue of an Orc, his expression faded away, and was followed by the entry of Lucius.

"Did you find the queen?" he asked Marcus, then he looked at me "oh, thank god my queen, please don't wander of next time," and then he saw the statue of the Orc, "HOLY MOTHER OF THE KNIGHTS OF THE ROUND TABLE, WHAT IN THE NAME OF THE BEARD OF THE HOLY KNIGHT IS A DEAD ORC DOING HERE?"

Then Marcus asked me "My queen, did you slay this monster?"

I was very shocked by the incident but somehow managed to nod to the question, Marcus and Lucius both nodded after looking at each other and quickly kneeled before me and said, "ALL HAIL THE PEACE-QUEEN, THE PROTECTER OF THE NATURE AND THE ORC-SLAYER"

Chapter 5

Confronting the Rock Giant

Ok now time for some heavy duty action of the strongest knight, if you like action, this chapter will make superheroes look like a pansy, so read on..............

"I am sorry, I never meant to do this, I was just trying to stall him so that I can run away, I never wanted to kill him" I cried, I just couldn't stop myself from grieving, it felt pretty awful to learn that I had to kill someone (more like 'Something') so that I could protect myself, you know, I am just an ordinary teenager, who never needed to kill anyone back on earth, right?

Marcus held my hand and soothingly said "My queen, your actions were executed because of the rash and wrong intentions of the Orc, had he understood the importance of his victim, he may have thought twice before engaging, but nonetheless, his death is nothing but a trivial issue when compared to your duty for the whole parallel universe of living beings."

He clearly wanted to cheer me up, but this wasn't going to help me in one bit.

I killed someone, and the emotions were out of the charts. Both of them tried to consolidate me, I knew that they wanted me to enjoy the moment as I was strong enough to protect myself. Somehow, I controlled my emotions, and tried to feel better, I mean, it not every day when you realize that you are as strong as a superhero, right?

We all got back to our camp, where Marcus had laid a sleeping sack for me, it was like a vegetable sack, just a bit bigger with a small cotton pillow attached to it from the outside, it wasn't looking any good, but when I laid down, I felt as if I am lying over a cotton ball, and maybe that's why when I closed my eyes, I quickly went to sleep.

Then again, I had the most weird dream I could ever think of, I couldn't see anything clearly, but I was not alone, though the place was so foggy that I could hardly see what is happening over a couple of meter, but then, suddenly, the ground beneath me started shaking, and a big, and by big I mean COLOSSAL, being emitted from the ground, as if it was a zombie or something, it was very big, so big that it will make a skyscraper look like a dollhouse or something.

In front of it was an average sized boy, I couldn't see anything about him apart from his size, though by his posture he looked as if he wasn't afraid.

They both stared at each other, then the colossal zombie thing tried to punch the boy by lifting its hand, and the boy ran with great speed towards the punch.

He jumped, and contracted his power in his fist, and when their punches collided then a big explosion took place, as if a nuclear bomb or a hydrogen bomb exploded, the explosion was coming near me, but I could not move, I was stuck to the ground!

I tried to move my legs, but then I realized that they are deep stuck in the earth below me, and as the explosion reached me, I closed my eyes, and everything went blank.

I felt as if there was a sticky liquid on my face, I opened my eyes, and then I saw, Fang was licking up my face!!!

"EW!!!' the only word that could come out of my mouth at that time. I mean, I hate when someone wakes me up before I want to, and this was the first time when a giant wolf did by licking me! Yuck, mega yuck!!!

I saw that Marcus and Lucius were already up and ready, they were discussing about the rest of the trips by reading a couple of maps and examining them. Then their eyes got at me.

"Oh so fang woke you up I suppose?" Lucius said

"You think?" I replied sarcastically (what do you expect, I was mad, I mean, my eyes are open in surprise, my sleep was ruined, I was sleep deprived, and most of all, I was disturbed by giant wolf who LICKED ME, so yes, you can say that I was pretty mad.)

"The nightmare would have been better than this!" I snapped, and at this comment, both the knights' faces grew pale as they first saw each other, and then saw me.

"Did you have a vision, my queen?" Marcus asked me

"No, I just had the weirdest dream I ever could know of" I replied as I cleaned my face covered in saliva by my handkerchief.

"No, you do not seem to understand," Lucius added, "re-incarnations of the regal status, just like yourself, when are brought to their home planet, can see vision of the coming events, it mostly happens to warn about the near future, so please, if you saw anything, tell us"

"I don't remember actually, I don't remember most of the stuff" I admitted, "All I remember was to see a very giant, huge zombie kind of thing, and, in front of him was a normal person, they both maybe challenged each other for a fight, and then I woke up"

"Do you remember how the person looked" Marcus asked me.

"No, that's all I could see for the time being" I replied. Both the knights grew very alert, and started trying to find out the meaning of the vision/dream.

"We have a lot of work to do my friend" Marcus told Lucius.

"Yes Marcus, you try to find out the meaning of the vision, while I will fill up our water bottles, we will need it direly for our next place," Lucius replied.

"But try to understand, I cannot decipher the meaning without a scholar like you!" Marcus exclaimed.

"Guys, guys" I said trying to calm them down, "If my dream is something really important to do, then you ought to do it, I can fill up our water stock by myself"

"No my queen" Marcus protested, "we cannot risk your safety, not again, not now"

"Oh chill out dude" I said "I mean I will take my Lunar-ray (My specs that change into a knight's helmet) and my jacket with me ok" I wore my jacket to show him that now no harm would come to me. I also took my specs and put it in my jacket pocket.

"But, what if, another monster comes, bigger and stronger than the Orc?" he asked, "You won't be able to call out for even help"

"quit worrying, I'll take fang and the other unicorns with me, if I get busy in engaging a stronger monster, then they can run and inform you, right?"

Lucius thought for a second, then he whispered to Marcus, "giving away our only means of transportation to one who has a little experience of protecting herself, are you certain that this is the best idea?"

Marcus thought for a second, and then replied, "and what other alternative do we have, if you want to save time, and make it as fast as you can to reach the knight's stronghold Kingslograd, then I advise that we go by her way when it comes to save time"

After a little more discussion all of us agreed, and I took Fang, Noel and Phillip with me to the river side so that they all could quench their thirst too, both of the knight's hadn't given the animals water since the last night, this was the least I could do for them, in return to what they had done to protect me. I took all of them near the bank of the river, and let them have some fun, the unicorns started eating the wet grass of the river bank and Fang started sniffing around with his big nose, he was finding something.

I was too busy in filling up the water bottles, when suddenly, I saw that the unicorns lifted their heads in surprise, and fang, gave a little growl, and made an attacking posture. The unicorns started looking everywhere, as if they were trying to find something, and Fang, would not stop sniffing.

I understood that we were not alone, and someone was near, though I was still not sure whether it was a threat or not. But to take a measurable precaution, I wore my knight helmet, and jacket armor.

Then, just like the last night, someone said in familiar tone, "Going so soon?"

And I knew who it was, it was the same ENT, who met me last night and helped me in solving my questions.

"So it is you, and I was so afraid that another Orc will show up!" I transformed my lunar ray back into my specs, and said, "So, tell me one more thing, will you?"

I wanted him to help me one last time in knowing what will happen, if everything goes on as correctly as planned. But both the knights were not going to open up their mouths, so I had to make do with this freaking talking tree!!

But before I could even ask anything, Fang growled at the old Ent and the unicorns came in from of me, as if they were trying to protect me or something. Fang started barking at the Ent, and the unicorns lifted their first two hooves.

It was looking as if the job of the unicorns was to protect me, and the job of Fang was to fight the Ent, Even though both of them were not having any arms!

"My queen" the Ent said in an uncomfortable tone, "What could have I possibly done to deserve such aggression?" his weary eyes were very frightened, and I never wanted him to die.

"Fang!" I shouted, "What are you doing, stop it, he means us no harm!"

The gigantic wolf stared at me, and raised his eyebrow (though he was not having any) as if saying 'you sure about this?'

"Yes, guys, I am totally sure that Mr. Ent here is going to help us" I said, though the animals were calm now, but we had lost our fun, the unicorns started eating grass again, but Fang stayed beside me, like a faithful dog, he sat down, and was very alert.

The Ent, who finally felt secured, got back his senses.

"I am sorry for the little scenario back there" I apologized to him, "The guys, are a little over protective, but I had no idea that the animals will be too!"

"I can understand your highness" He said, "the animals of this dimensions, though have the same intelligence as THE animals you have in yours, here, they are capable and more comfortable when it comes to understanding the emotions and the needs of their masters."

"Yeah I just saw that, you know" I said.

"By the way, I presume that your majesty needed another explanation for her question?"

"Ah yes," I said, as finally we were on the right topic, "I just wanted to know, if you are ok with it, that to tell me, what will happen, if, everything goes just as planned by the prophecy"

The Ent seemed to be a puzzled after hearing this question but then said, "I am sorry your highness, but I can be of no service in this subject"

"Why," I exclaimed, "I mean, you are supposed to be the smartest one here, then why can't you tell me what will happen if everything goes as planned?"

"I cannot tell you whether your coming to the throne will be the hope for the universe, or end of the worlds" the Ent answered back in a grave tone, "I know not even if you a meant to survive this journey, I know not, because no one else knows, in the books these few days, are called as the 'Judgment time' marked by all the gods from all mythologies, to check whether the re-incarcerated one has a soul pure enough and good enough that she can ascend to the throne which will help in protecting the humanity of all the dimensions, or will it be, the end, so that the gods get a clean slate to start life once again"

This was frigging ridiculous, literally after all this rescuing and giving super strength kind of power, I get to hear, 'oh so you are going on a journey of no return, good, very good, by the way just for the memo, you'll end up blowing the whole universe, or maybe if you are lucky enough, you will live to see it, good luck!!'

Then the Ent continued, "But the recent transformation that you have got is the most big deciding factor, tell me my queen, had you any dreams or visions of some sort?"

"Yes!" I cried out happily "yes, I had a dream, and even Marcus and Lucius said that it was a vision, but what do you think, does this make sense?" I asked.

"curious," he said, "the most curious indeed, well if you don't mind, shall I understand what the dream was meant for"

"No luck" I explained it to him, "Both of the knights are still trying to figure out what does this means, but I don't think that they will be going anywhere"

"No you don't seem to understand," he replied, "I won't need you to tell me about the dream, I shall find it by myself, I must enter your brain and try to decipher the meaning"

"wait a second," I snapped, "You will enter my brain! No way I can't let you read my thoughts, and what if you mess up my mind, then who's to blame?"

"My queen, the Ents have been known to the entire kingdom about their greatness in mind reading, I give you my word that no harm will come to you, and moreover, I shall not look anyway beyond of what you seek to know, your thoughts and perception are safe with you."

"Ok, well, try not to fry up my brain ok" I warned him, "Fry it up and Fang will use you as a toothpick, isn't that right?" I said as I looked at the giant wolf. Fang looked at me, and then after realizing that it was just a joke, started wagging his tail.

"Thank you for the kind warning my queen" The Ent said.

"No I was just kidding, but try not to go any bit further ok" I said,

"Very well" he said, "Now I would like you to close your eyes and concentrate at the vision that you dreamed of."

I did as he told me, and I somehow, I found myself right where I was in my dream. The place was all same, everything was very foggy, and I could hardly see further than 7 to 8 meters.

Suddenly everything that happened to me in my vision, started taking place, the land was shattering, the ground was shaking, the ground beneath me was being torn up, and was shattered.

Then, I saw that as the land trembled, that a huge colossal human figure came out as if a huge zombie came out of a grave. The huge monster was, well HUGE!

Then just as I thought another person, who was human, was just in front of the monster, he ran and contracted all his power in his fist, and it stared glowing, his fist was glowing silver! The monster charged at him and lifted his hand to hit him

Their fist collided together and once again, a huge explosion took place, but this time, I could run away from it. But I wasn't so lucky.

The speed of the explosion was so fast that I knew that I was going to die unless a miracle happens, and somehow, my wish got true! I saw that nearby was a portal, when I ran near it, I saw that there were our unicorns, Fang, and the Ent, there was even my body, and I was in a deep sleep. Then I realized that all of this is actually happening in my mind!

I rushed for the portal, but, then I saw that the fire of the explosion is closing in. I started running even faster, but the wave could still outrun me, with the last ounce of energy left in me I jumped towards the portal, I could feel the heat of the blast, but then as I came near, and got inside the portal, everything went black once again.

As I opened my eyes, I saw that I was laying down on the ground, Fang was sniffing me, as if checking whether I am alive or not, both of the unicorns were gathered around me, and the Ent was very worried. As I stood up, his face lit up.

"Ah, my queen, I was very worried," He confessed, "I thought as if I lost you, as if I just threw the worlds into oblivion, you were in great danger indeed, but you should thank your stars that you came back alive"

"Yeah, I think I should" I said, "So tell me, what did you see?"

The Ent's facial expressions told me that something nasty was about to happen, "I hoped that I had more good news, but I apologize. Though you saw what you had seen in the vision, I saw what was necessary,"

He became more serious and his tone became more grave, "Listen to me my queen, the monster that you are going to face today, is by no means low in standards, it is an elemental, and represents earth, no one can destroy him apart from the supreme knight, mark my words, do not engage with him, and don't let the elite knight as well, only Marcus can tackle him, do you understand?"

"Yes sure," I said, "I will not do anything today, and I also wanted to see how strong Marcus actually is, so you know, I think that I will get a chance to see him in action"

The Ent smiled and said, "Don't take the supreme knights as low in power, they are just as strong as they are rare, they can lift mountains, tame seas, even destroy an entire civilizations, so do not take them lightly"

Then he added, "You must go on my lady, time is less, and we have already made it lesser, go on, if fate has this in its way, our paths shall cross once again, I hope,"

"I hope for the same," I replied, "You helped me a lot, thanks for that"

"I was just doing my duty, your majesty," he said, "farewell"

"Goodbye" I replied as I took Fang and the unicorns back to the camp.

"Are you alright your majesty?" Lucius asked, "You took so long that we were afraid that you might not show up."

Both of them were ready for travelling, they packed their bags, and our beds, Lucius had prepared some food and Marcus took care of all the maps and other stuff.

"You sound just like my parents" I replied back, "Quit worrying, I can handle myself, thanks to you guys and the arsenal"

"I see" Lucius said, "well, I think we ought to go now, we can't afford to stay any bit longer."

"You are right" Marcus added, "Now, we must move on." Both of them hanged their sacks on the animals, and then we went on. It took us at least 2 hours before we crossed the 'Beatle woods'. I saw that now we were once again surrounded by large prairie grasslands.

There was an old board which was pointing in a direction and on it was written "𝕾𝖆𝖓𝖉𝖊𝖗 𝕷𝖆𝖓𝖉𝖘 𝖔𝖋 𝖙𝖍𝖊 𝕹𝖔𝖗𝖙𝖍"

It was then that the animals picked up their speed. As the distant to be covered was large, and as the grasslands were free of obstacles, the unicorns showed their true speed. Fangs speed was remarkable, he was almost five to six meters away from us and our unicorns were right behind him.

I was very astonished to see that the unicorns were not a bit tired even though they had run miles and miles on foot, and they were still galloping as if they were not tired at all. The wind that was blowing due to the speed of Noel was astonishing, she was galloping so fast that I felt as if I am driving a bike without wearing a helmet, it was difficult for me to even breath properly, and as riding on unicorns was not my best subject, I had difficulty in balancing myself, but I managed just fine.

After once again riding for 5 to 6 hours, we all took a break for 15 minutes. I was so tired after riding on Noel, that my hands were starting to ache, and I was so thirsty that I finished one water bottle in one go. Even the knights were so thirsty that they drank all the water in their bottles. Then after this, Marcus and Lucius were trying to find directions. After literally guessing that we were not lost, we started moving again.

Then again after a couple of hours later, as we galloped our way through the grasslands, I saw that we were approaching fast towards a place where half of the land was full of big hills and there the prairie are was much less than what was here.

As we got near the place, I saw that there was a board where it was written, '𝔇𝔢𝔯𝔢𝔨𝔲𝔰 𝔥𝔦𝔩𝔩𝔰 𝔬𝔣 𝔊𝔞𝔩𝔡𝔞𝔯𝔱𝔥'

Marcus looked at the sign board and said, "Yes, we have followed the map correctly my friend, we should go now, I want to cross these hills and cliffs before nightfall"

"I wished to be the bearer of good news Marcus" Lucius interrupted, "But, our water stock is almost extinguished, we do not have more than half of water bottle more to quench our thirst!"

"I can understand." He replied, "but, we cannot afford to stay here for any longer, we have to make haste, though if somehow, there is a small lake or any water body, then we can fill our bottles there"

As we moved on, the scenic beauty totally changed, on my right side, were the long prairies, which were hardly having any tree or shelter of some kind, whereas on my left hand side, there were huge hills and cliffs, some attached together through hundreds and thousands of years while some were big enough to make themselves look as if they are joined.

In other words, those hills resembled just like the place 'Grand Canyon'

Lucius told me that these hills could go over 400 meters high, and that just like a tree, the foundation of these hills were buried deep beneath the surface, which could be deep down to almost 200 meters. I was so engrossed in watching the scenic beauty that I hardly felt a tremor that took place underneath the ground.

"Did you feel that?" Lucius warned me.

"UH!? What happened?" I said, I hate to be a very bad observant, but, I can't help it. Then, again, another tremor took place. This time, it was different; it was much more shocking than the last one.

Then a series of tremors started shocking the whole place, the animals were not able to balance themselves, it was very hard to balance their bodies.

"Lucius take her majesty to safety!" shouted Marcus, "I shall deal with what is happening here"

He got down from Fang, and ordered him to get away as quickly as he can, though Fang was reluctant to go at first, but then he had to follow his master's orders, so he led the way, as I and Lucius followed him to safety, while Marcus stayed behind.

It took us some time but then, we were at least a 5 kilometers away from the spot.

"What will happen to Marcus?" I asked Lucius.

"Nothing My dear lady," Lucius replied, "He is the supreme knight, there is no one stronger than them in this universe, and he can handle whatever is causing the tremors."

I took out Lunar ray, and wore it. I quickly zoomed on the zone where Marcus was standing. I was shocked that I could see so far from my helmet, it was as if I was watching some sort of 3-D television.

I saw that it was difficult for Marcus to keep his balance, he was constantly trying to stand on his feat, but it was very difficult. The tremors were so devastating that a lot of hills were falling down, and among them, the biggest one was having the most problem, it was shaking very badly.

But it was a little later that I saw that, the tremors weren't causing the hill to shake so badly, it was the HILL itself that was causing the tremors to take place!!!

"How is this even possible?" I asked Lucius, "How can a hill cause an earthquake like that!" this stuff was literally way too much for me, I couldn't handle anymore of this.

"The only logical explanation my queen," Lucius replied as he wore his helmet, "Is because that is not a hill, it is a giant, THE ROCK GIANT"

And as he finished his sentence, the hill lifted itself up so strongly that it shocked the ground all the way till here! And then, came the tough part. The hill lifted itself up slowly, and actually what we were thinking a hill was actually the 'Back' of a colossal giant! He shoved his lower part with other hills and merged them with himself making them his legs. He took what were his shoulders and slammed it on other hills, merging and making it his arms and hands.

And then the Monster got up. It was a colossal being who was so big that it will make Godzilla look like his small brother. His upper body added a head, which slowly and slowly started getting full of expressions. As I zoomed it, I saw two brown eyes, a big nose, and a beard, a big beard.

He was a colossal monster made up of rock!

The data that Lunar ray gave me was like this,

SPECIES: ROCK GIANT

RANK: A GRADE

HIEGHT: 1200 feet

INTERESTS: USUALY SLEEPING UNDERNEATH THE GROUND, ARE VERY PEACEFUL AND MAKE NO THREATS, BUT CAN BECOME A DEVASTATING FORCE WHEN ANGERED.

There were many questions that were occurring in my mind, such as, "Did we make him angry, how can we make him so mad that he destroys an entire zone!" or "How the hell are we going to beat him, just look at him, 1200 feet! How the hell can we beat him?"

And then it hit me, the huge zombie which came underneath from the ground, was actually 'the Rock Giant!' He is the 'Elemental' who came to destroy me, and, the other guy is Marcus, the supreme knight, who fights him, HOLY COW, now, what will happen!

Marcus wore his read helmet. His helmet transformed very slowly, as if showing of its way. Marcus was not looking one bit afraid of what was standing in front of him. And neither was Lucius afraid to see what his friend is going up against.

"What is your demand My giant friend?" asked Marcus looking at him.

The Rock Giant said something that I could not understand, "zhe ist ma no le ga karozte!"

Marcus heard him for a while then he said, "I am sorry My friend, but I am afraid that it is not possible.

You see, the queen holds the key to our salvation, and I can't let the key get into wrong hands you know."

The Rock giant said once again, "rae mo end fjae iniem jhifa baek dingoz la bea no diz ga fed!"

"I can understand, but I want to tell you that violence cannot sort this up," He said in a very friendly manner, "I don't want to destroy an elemental like you, but, I promise you that if you go back to sleep now, and let us pass, then you will be unharmed"

Before Marcus could even wait for a reply, the giant lifted his big fist, and slammed at Marcus. But the supreme knight saw this and dodged his fist very easily, and landed a few yards away from the place.

"I don't want to kill you, don't make me" He warned.

But the rock giant wouldn't listen, he tried to slam him again, and Marcus dodged him once again.

"Alright," he said, "You wanted to challenge me, so be it," he was ready for the next attack, as the rock giant hit him; he quickly dodged it, and landed on his hand. Before the Rock giant could find where his tiny opponent was, Marcus who was on the Giant's neck, landed a strong blow right on his face.

The force was strong enough to crack his whole face, the rock giant though was surprised, but wasn't beaten. Just as Marcus was in midair, preparing to land on ground, the Rock giant punched him so hard, that Marcus flew at least a mile away from the zone.

His force was so strong that even though when Marcus managed to land on his feat, he was being dragged by the force; he had to slam his fist against the ground to stop him from being dragged.

As Marcus stood up, the rock giant, Lifted an entire hill, (which was actually huge) and threw it at Marcus. The supreme knight did nothing, apart from placing his forearms in front of his chest, and braced for impact. The hill came closer and closer as my breathing grew faster.

And finally the hill collided right on him! He did nothing apart from bracing for impact! I was shocked, was this the end of Marcus, I mean, he was supposed to save me, according to my Vision, was this all a lie all along, was Marcus not that strong, was he not worthy enough, and strong enough to beat the rock giant?

The questions were once again filling up in my mind when suddenly I heard someone giggling.

I looked back, and I saw that it was Lucius! He wasn't sad in the least to see his friend get squashed up.

"Why the hell are you laughing? Now what will we do?" I exclaimed at him.

Lucius, after managing to stop his laughing said, "I am sorry your majesty, I am actually laughing on the stupidity of the Rock giant."

UH? This was the thought that occurred inside my brain.

"I see that the giant thinks that this small attack can stop the supreme knight! What is this, it's just a hill, nothing else, he can withstand at least thousand times more than this!" he replied.

And as his sentence was finished I saw that the hill which was on Marcus, started shaking, and the shaking grew faster each second!

And just after the 5 seconds, the whole hill was smashed to bits as Marcus unleashed his power. I saw that he was not having any trouble doing that, he was still very calm; he was actually trying not to hurt his opponent.

But the rock giant was not sharing the same mercy that Marcus had for him. The Rock Giant was getting frustrated. I could see the tension in his eyes, even though I did not know his language. With one last straw to kill Marcus, he started running towards him.

I was not able to stop thinking that what will be his next move. Then all of a sudden, the giant who was almost halfway till Marcus, Jumped! He squeezed his legs and pushed himself upward! His power was almost so much that he could almost touch the sky!

I mean, he was like, over 1200 feat! And could weigh almost half a billion ton! How the hell is he strong enough to jump that high! But it was later that I realized what were his true motives. As he was falling down, he aimed at Marcus and smashed right on him!!!

His landing was so strong that it actually caused an earthquake for at least half a minute. I was misbalanced because of all this shaking of the ground beneath my feet.

At first, I once again started thinking that Marcus couldn't have survived that blow, but then, I saw that the giant was shaking, and even he didn't know why, I zoomed as much as I could, and I saw that it was Marcus! He was lifting the rock giant, and even the giant was exerting force on his feet, Marcus was able to lift him!

Marcus lifted the rock giant, and slammed him on the earth. I could hear the sound of the hills felling down till here. The scene was really sensational. I never had seen something s epic.

Rock giant somehow maintained his balance, and then saw that Marcus wasn't even tired, or anything what you will expect him to happen after a fight. He was just watching the giant as if trying to tell him that what grave mistake he was doing.

The Rock giant, in mad desperation, didn't know what to do, his strength was clearly outmatched. All he could do was to punch his opponent. He just punched him with everything he had got. He hit Marcus with so much brute strength that he was again dragged by the force, the giant was constantly punching Marcus, he didn't knew what to do.

And Marcus becoming angry with each blow, he wanted to be left peacefully and what did he got in return, PUNCHES FROM A WALKING MOUNTAIN!!!

Finally when the Rock Giant punched him for one last time, Marcus shouted "Enough!" As the rock giant hit him, Marcus grabbed the giant's huge fist, lifted it, and with it, he lifted the giant himself.

He lifted and lifted till the whole body of the giant was in the air. Then, when Marcus reached half way in the air, then he slammed the colossal body to the ground!

"Here my queen, you will see the true power of the supreme knight!" shouted Lucius in excitement!

Marcus jumped as high as he could. He was at least 900 feet in the air, (according to lunar ray). He contracted all his power in his fist and shouted "FIST OF LIGHTENING!" and as he said this, the lightening strikes in the air covered his fist, and as he fell down, on his fist, he slammed it against the body of the Rock Giant.

As his fist slammed on the giant's body, a shockwave was emitted by the powerful impact of the punch. The shockwave was so big that it resembled the nuclear explosion which happened in my dream. It was so big that it came all the way till me. Lucius had to cover me so that I won't be harmed by the shockwave. It was so strong that it went over 3 miles farther than where we were standing.

Just as everything was cleared, I saw that nothing was left of the rock Giant, apart from some debris and rubble, and from within the thick layer of dust, came out Marcus. He was very calm as if nothing happened, and was walking towards us.

Fang ran towards his master and licked him as he got there. Marcus had to order him to stop this. Then on Fang he covered the rest of the distance till he reached near us.

"The bigger they are" he said, "the harder they fall"

"Was that your true power? Did you kill him?" I asked him excitedly.

"Well, actually today, I was rather in a jolly good mood, and I never wanted to hurt the rock giant on purpose, but then, yes, you can say that you have seen my power. And as for killing him, I just disintegrated him, his remains are still on the surface of Galdarth, so being an elemental, he will heal itself through time, but it will take some time, say 2 to 3 months."

My brain once again went in a buffering mode. I just saw one of the most awesome gigantic fights in my life and the fighter here says that he was in a good mood that is why he decimated his opponent with such brute strength.

"So, shall we move on?" asked Marcus. And both I and Lucius got on our respected unicorns. Then once again our journey started.

Chapter 6

History of Marcus

This chapter has a bit less action, it is kind of like part love story, part tragedy, part action, so readers you are going to like this part.......

We rode all the way from the fighting zone, and rode till the dusk of the day. After reaching as a specific place, all of us got down our animals, and the knights started preparing for food. It was a very good move of Lucius that he had packed the fruits from the other day.

But, we still needed fire, without it, we won't be able to see a darn thing of our surroundings. And none of us was not in a mood to wear the helmet so that it may help us in seeing through night-vision.

"You may rest now Lucius," Marcus said, "we have had a very busy day, I shall collect the firewood this time, and I will try to find a water body, if there is any nearby."

"But Marcus" Lucius protested, "the victory which you have achieved today is far more than what I have done; you ought to rest right now, not me."

"And yes one more thing Lucius" he replied, "That is an order"

Lucius could do nothing apart from watching his courteous friend work hard to find wood. Marcus took all the empty water bottles and went inside those hills wearing his helmet. We both saw him as he went forth and disappeared among the hills.

"So, I think now will be a good time to help him by laying the bed" Lucius suggested.

"Yeah," I chimed in, "I guess so"

We both laid out our beds, with the bed for Marcus. According to Lucius Marcus had done a great deal of work today by defeating the Rock Giant. Yeah, he really did. It is not every day you see a boy lifting almost a billion ton walking MOUNTAIN!

"So" I said, "I guess I owe Marcus a thanks, he saved my life back there."

"Though he did" Lucius replied as he took out some bed sheets from the sack on Philip (His unicorn), "But he won't accept it, according to him, he was just doing his job, you owe him nothing, and he will gladly give his life for you." He laid the bed sheets on each of our beds, as he finished his sentence.

"Yeah but" I replied, "There is still something that is bothering me you know"

"And what is that dear lady?"

"How come Marcus knew that he was the one who was supposed to fight the Rock Giant?" I asked.

"That is a very good question My queen" he said, "Well at first you may think that my answer is a bit unnatural but what if, I tell you that Fang gave us the details of the talks that you did with the Ent?"

"So you are saying that the Big wolf can talk?" I asked gritting my teeth as it really was very stupid.

"No" He replied calmly, "We agreed to send Fang with you as he could tell Marcus what had happened during the secret experiment with the Ent. Though Fang cannot speak, his only master Marcus can understand what he means to say, they both are somehow connected, just like you are with Noel, and I am with Philip."

Though at first I thought that this was all foolish but then it started making sense, when I first came here, then I could understand what Noel wanted to convey to me. Maybe he was right after all. So I decided to drop the subject.

Then after some time Lucius gave me some fruits to eat, it was just about to get dark, and the sky was now turning from red to dark blue slowly. We both sat together while eating our dinner, Lucius saved some for Marcus, and placed them in his sack.

"Tell me Lucius" I said, "it is almost 2 days since I am here, and I hardly know about you two guys"

"What do you mean?" he asked, as he finished eating his apple.

"I mean that I want to know about your history, Marcus's History, can you tell it to me if this doesn't bothers you?" I said, "Like how old are you?"

"I am over 183 years old if we consider it with your world, while Marcus is also 183" He replied.

"Wait, say what" I said shockingly, "183 years old, you guys don't look older than a teenager, and you guys look like you are in your mid teens!"

"Yes, I can understand your astonishment, but we knights keep our youth for longer so that we can fight for a long time." He took out a small flask having purple water and said, "we have to drink this water each year so that we can keep our youthfulness for as long as we want, and if we don't, then we start aging normally."

"Whoa, my mom seriously needs some of that" I said slyly.

"I beg your pardon?"

"oh, nothing, just nothing, so you were telling me about your history weren't you?" I said trying to change the topic.

"Yes why not" he replied, "I was born to a peasant family we were a little well of, who when I was just a couple of weeks old, adopted Marcus, who was a couple of days old. We both lost our mother at a very early age. We later joined the Royal Knight Academy for warriors, and that is how we ended up like this."

"That's it?" I exclaimed, "this can't be all! I mean it has to be more"

"Oh so you wish to know everything," Lucius said, "well, it is good for you as I am also known as Lucius the 'Story-teller'. So let us start from the beginning shall we, would you mind if I tell you this story in my way?" And then Lucius started to tell me about their history.

And now his story goes like this: (seriously guys, the first part might be a little boring, but it goes nice later, so please don't skip it, thanks, its Lucius speaking for heaven's sake)

No one knows Marcus better than I do; we lived in the same house.

It was almost 183 years ago, it was midnight, and the moon was in its full shape. As the clock struck at the 12th hour, the cries a newborn baby echoed through the walls of a very poor slum. The mother happiness knew no bounds to see her infant son alive and well in her weak arms.

The child smiled at the first sight, it was a rare moment as infants that small cannot smile, and 'the child is destined for glory' said one of the barmaids, who were watching the sight.

But alas, though mother was happy to bear her first child, she knew that she could not see her child grow up as a man. The pain was too much for her, and she kissed him on his forehead, and whispered, "You are destined for greatness indeed" and died.

The father who was watching didn't know what to do, be happy that he is a father, or grieve as he had lost his love of life. Before the conclusion came in his mind, several lights started emitting from the shadows of the forest. They all were flickering, and if they were fireflies, but the fireflies aren't so big. The light was flickering and waving, and it was growing bigger in size as they drew nearer.

At first the father grew cautious but later gave a sign of relieve when he realized that they were just little forest fairies holding their small sparkling wands. They had come to give their blessings to the child, for they had read the ancient scriptures and knew what the child was destined for.

The seven prime Fairy Godmothers came to give their blessings to the infant, who gave a beautiful smile after watching the fairies. Each of them gave the child the best of all the blessings they had reserved for someone special.

Then came the father, who said "I have not any supernatural thing to give to you, but as your father, all I can give you at the moment, is a name" he looked at his wife's lifeless body and said, "we had an agreement that I will name you as you are our first born, but as you resemble my wife, and your mother, I will give you the name she wanted, I proclaim you Marcus! My only heir"

The heart of the father was large, but his deeds were small. He was a poor peasant, who now had more burden as he had a child to feed and had lost his wife. Knowing this, the fairies went beside the stressed father and told him, "Angus, listen to us, you have not the proper means of upbringing this infant, and he will perish even before he becomes a toddler!"

"You have to give the boy to someone who can give him a proper upbringing, and who can send him to the academy of the knights. You have your own duties as a peasant, and now you have a burden of caring for the child, you can't do both things, The future of Galdarth is dependent on him" they continued.

The father was reluctant at first, for it will mean that he may never see his child again. But then when the fairies told him about his destiny, the father made sure that nothing would make the child sad during the trip.

The fairies told Angus that he must let the child travel alone, so that he can reach at the right place, and the safest way was to depart him on the holy river called "River Of Hopes".

But the father was so poor that he could not even charter a boat, so he came up with a plan, he find out a basket big enough to handle the baby. He gave all the milk he had left from the cow and placed it in the basket.

Just as the new morning came, Angus was ready to bid farewell to his son, he placed his infant son in the basket. Some fairies who were present at the moment, cast a spell which will make the boy sleep till he finds a right home.

He took a sheet of paper, and wrote on it, "Marcus, My heir is now in your protection, keep him well." And then as he placed the basket on the slowly flowing water of the river, the basket went on it gently.

The father could not bear to watch his child go away at this young age, so he started crying, but the fairies supported him by telling that his sacrifice will not go in vain.

Mean while the child who was sound asleep, did not come to know of the path. The river took him far away, through valleys and forests and mountains, till he reached at a village called 'Rubegart'.

There, a woman who was washing her clothes came to be in the possession of the child. The child awoke from his sleep, and not looking at a familiar face, started wailing. She quickly fetched the milk in the basket, and fed it to the baby.

Then she waited and waited for someone who could be looking for the infant, but no one came. Then just as she saw the baby's smile, she made a decision that changed her fate, she adopted the boy. The woman was no one else than my mother.

Before leaving, she took the basket with herself and came to her house. "Adam," asked the young lady, "how many children do we have?"

"Merida" he replied, "we have one, our Lucius"

She showed him the baby with the basket and said, "Now we have two"

My father was delighted to see another young baby at his doorstep. He quickly went to the barn and decided to make another cradle for him.

"So what shall we call him?" My Father asked.

"I found this note in the basket, and it says, that his name is Marcus" My mother answered, "what a wonderful name it is, isn't it Adam. I wonder what happened to his parents"

And so Marcus was invited open heartedly in my family. I still remember the first time I saw him. We both looked at each other through our cradle, and at that precise moment, we became the best friends one could ever dream of.

We would play together, eat together, sleep together, oh god at one time, we even wished to go to the toilet together to check whose poop smells worse!

From the time we could read, all we both ever wanted to become was a knight of arms. We dreamed of it, and so after saving enough money, my parents could afford to send us to the Royal Knight Academy.

We both went to the academy when we were 12 years old.

When we first reached to Kingslograd, I was a bit nervous, we always lived in a small village where the houses were small and the people did small jobs, but as we entered the gates of the city, I started sweating.

There were houses made up of bricks and mortar and wood, unlike back in our village where people use either wood or just brick. There were banks and big market, libraries, schools, shops, and good amount of beautiful monuments. But the most beautiful one was the biggest one, Castle Kingslograd, the stronghold of the knights.

People were wearing rich clothes and everyone had a regal nature. They moved with a purpose, yet they smiled as if they are enjoying every morsel of the sweet life. And this made me a little nervous, I was never a very confident person, I never liked big regal people, and here was a city full of them!

But Marcus was enjoying his ride on the Unicorn-cart. He always loved challenges, and he was desperate to learn the way of the knights. And so as we both entered the gates of the castle, we sealed our fate.

Lucius stopped his story at that point. But I knew that he was concealing something from me, and I had to know it.

"That's it!" I demanded, "that can't be it"

"No, this is it, we started training and we became what we are today, the end" he replied.

"Come on give me a break" I snapped, "I was beginning to enjoy the story now, and you had to stop it" then suddenly, an idea struck my mind.

"I thought you were called Lucius 'The story Teller'" I started playing, "I think that you lied to me, it was just an exaggeration, wasn't it?"

"It was not" Lucius just lost his temper, "Oh queen you are lucky to be of great need or if it would have been someone else, I would have punched him so hard that it would make sure that he never see the sunlight again."

"Why, truth hurts?" I snapped.

"It's not that" He replied, "I am sure that, you won't like what happens next, I just know it"

"How can we be sure unless you tell me?"

"I am a man of my word My Lady, and I am sure of it"

"Oh come on it won't be so bad, will it, I mean, what has this story got to do with me right?" I asked,

"You are saying it doesn't!" Lucius said, "You are the whole thing because of which this happened!"

"How do you know that?" I snapped.

"It is because it was YOU with whom Marcus fell in love with"

"He fell.... WHAT!" I cried.

"Yes, that's why you won't like this part, I am telling you." He said.

"HE DID NOT, HOW IS THIS EVEN POSSIBLE!" I shouted.

"What I mean my lady is that you were not even born by that time, your counterpart, or another life was present in this universe, her name was Marion. Who later became our peace queen, and that's whom Marcus fell in love with." He answered.

I gave a sigh of relief, I mean, ME 183 years old hag!! I really wanted to punch someone, it wasn't that bad though, like having a boyfriend who is so strong that he can make other girls crush look like ants. This wasn't that bad, but I still wasn't very satisfied. I am not beautiful, any person with even half a brain can tell that I am just above average, but well, you know, luck turns the tide really.

"Oh you really made me afraid" I sighed, "I thought you were saying that I am 183 years old."

"Oh, so does it means that you won't feel bad if I tell you what happens next?" he verified.

"Oh no, go on, spill the beans" I said acting as if nothing happened while in my heart, I was so happy to know that I had a super-cool boyfriend once, and my heart was pounding to know what happened next.

"Ok then" Lucius declared, "Here we go" (so, Lucius starts again)

We entered the hall of the knights, where our professors and instructors were ready to give us a tour of the place! It was a colossal castle, which had a fortress, a palace and an academy inside, and also had dozens of libraries. It had tall tower, whose tops were coated with gold, and it had a flag having the same emblem on it that we have on our armor-jacket.

We were given our books from the academies bookshop, and our courses were set. I was going to be a scholar knight, who ranges with fighting on field as well as in the art of healing, what doctors do in your world. While Marcus aimed directly to become an elite knight.

Being very friendly, both of us, quickly started making friends. But our luck wasn't that good in this subject, being from a lesser known and having less social status, we were being frowned upon by almost every student, but yes, it was almost.

Marcus and I suddenly caught up with Nortus, the Master student, and the highest ranked elite knight of his time. He was using his purple potion as he told us that his age is over 42, but because he became a knight, he got his potion. At that time we realized that after becoming a knight, you may get a chance to beat even death itself.

But we didn't think of that much, Nortus quickly became our good friend, and he helped us in improving our social status in the academy. He was a very charming person, and so was his elder brother Morpheus, both of them were handsome enough to steal every girl's heart, especially during parties, which took place every weekend.

The important thing was that it was some days later we came to know that Morpheus and Nortus were actually the sons of the old supreme knight Rigorad. He was almost 1800 years old, and was looking at least in his 70s by that time, though he was a supreme knight, he was the worst of them all.

We four used to spend time with each other whenever we got free, all of us would tell the tale of the first supreme knight Zarthur, and how he banished the evil dragon king Fafnir.

In your world Fafnir was the dragon in Viking mythology who was killed by Sigurd. But in our universe, Fafnir exists in the knights era, and is very much real.

All the fairytales that would make boys go wild. In our world, fairy tale is almost as real as traffic signs in yours my queen.

We would spend time in the library, or in the class, or in the field, four of us were almost inseparable, but yes, almost.

You see, Marcus, being an honor student in his class as well as in field, got nearer and nearer to his dream of becoming an elite knight. While I was the best in my subjects, and as I had taken a much simpler course, my fate was sealed.

But unfortunately, Marcus's Fate took a different turn just when he saw the face of Marion on that tower that day. She just like me came to learn the art of healing.

They both looked in each other's eyes, and I knew that problem will come. I know that no good ever comes in falling in love but naive Marcus didn't listen to me.

It was our third year, which was the last year, and after getting the result, we would get our position as a knight. I was ready for my tests, but I worried about Marcus, he would not attend his classes, would not do any good in his test, though he was still the best when it came to the physical test on field, but in class, Marcus was de-grading.

I knew where he was going, he always missed his classes and went to see his love, Marion, but little did he know the grave consequences of his acts.

The High Priest proclaimed that it would be Marion to be proclaimed the peace-queen of Galdarth, soon, and a low-life like Marcus was not supposed to ask her to marry him.

Rigorad was growing old, so soon, he proclaimed that his son, Morpheus, will take his place when he dies, and to keep his family tradition, he asked Marion, the Peace-queen to marry his son. As she was the peace-queen and his son was king going to be, he couldn't find a better match. They were going to be married on the same day on which Marion is proclaimed the peace-queen, and Morpheus is proclaimed the Supreme knight, and the king of Kingslograd.

Though Morpheus was happy after hearing his father, but Marion was not, she loved Marcus with all her heart and could not imagine how she could live with anyone else. At the same time, Marcus lost his trust on Marion as she didn't tell him that she is going to be the peace-queen.

So, on the eve of their wedding, when everyone was jolly happy apart from Marcus, me and Marion, we came up with a plan. The plan was that Marion would tell everyone who her true love is when she is proclaimed the Peace-queen. And as even a supreme knight has no command over the queen, no one could go against her. It was very simple until Morpheus heard us.

His rage knew no bounds when he heard that we were plotting against him, and he was ravaging mad when he heard that Marion is amongst us.

He stopped the wedding eve's party, and challenged Marcus to a duel till death; the winner shall proclaim Marion as his bride.

But as Marcus tests were not near, he was not in a position to fight against a strong elite knight. But, it was arranged, Rigorad, who was amused to see fight between two knights quickly signed the form and made Marcus an elite knight. And within next half an hour, everything was set.

The clock struck one hour before midnight, and Morpheus started decimating Marcus. He was so angry that he could not even think that he was fighting his friend. Marcus, who never wanted to fight, was trying to calm his friend turned foe, so that everything can be at peace again. But Morpheus was not going to hear anything.

Morpheus was punching Marcus, and Marcus couldn't do anything. He never wanted to hurt his friend but then even he got angry. As Morpheus Punched him, he blocked it, and gave a counter punch with such brute strength that it made Morpheus fly away. Marcus grab holds of a tree, lifts it and uses it as his weapon hitting Morpheus again and again till the tree is destroyed.

Next thing I see is that Morpheus starts laughing, and says, "Now we will have a good fight."

Morpheus jumps as high as he could and jumped down at Marcus, though Marcus dodges his punch, but it destroys the ground where the punch landed. And so a fierce fight between two elite knights erupts, a fight so rare that you cannot see it again. It was first of its kind, a knight against a knight.

At first both of them had equal chances of winning, but then slowly but surely, Morpheus started taking the upper hand. Though Marcus was quite a challenge, but Morpheus had more experience as he actually served in the battle field for a couple of decades, and had fought demons, monsters and vandals, so he was holding an upper hand at the fight.

While Marcus hardly had any experience, and soon he started getting tired. I could see that his armor jacket was starting to tear off. And I knew he could no longer keep up with the stamina of his opponent Morpheus. And then Marcus, fell down on his knees, he could not handle the pain any more.

Morpheus started laughing, and started criticizing him, calling him by names, and said, "is that it? Is that all that you have got?" he kicked Marcus so hard that he went breaking away the walls of at least 5 building nearby.

Morpheus said, "Come on, show me more, I want a fight, you are nothing you mangy cur!" he continued saying, "you are a low-life dreaming of being a high profile knight, but in reality, you are not more than the dust beneath my shoes!"

He begins to punch Marcus, in order to end his life, when suddenly Marion comes in between them. She begs, and pleads with Morpheus to leave Marcus and says that she loves him truly and not Morpheus. She will take him as a very good friend and will forget about the incident if Morpheus just stop hurting Marcus.

But Morpheus, without thinking, in pure rage, hits poor Marion as she breaks the castle wall and struggles not to die. This incident shocked Marcus, to his core. It made him so angry that I saw a demon in his eyes.

"Yes, fight me; I want you to get angry!! Fight me!!!" Morpheus still keeps on challenging Marcus.

He keeps on shouting "Fight me, Hit me, and try to hit me if you dare"

And then he says for the last time "HIT ME" when Marcus hits Morpheus so hard that it emits a shock wave and breaks Morpheus's neck, resulting in his end. He slowly turns into a statue, and then Marcus punches it so hard that it is decimated and the Morpheus's statue is turned into dust.

In front of the whole street, in front of the knight's palace, in front of Rigorad the supreme knight, Marcus killed his dear son, in front of Nortus the master elite knight, Marcus killed his dear brother. Marcus lost his temper and killed his own brother in arms, such was the brutality done by his hands.

After realizing what he had done, he couldn't stop but cry, he never intended to kill his friend, but he left him no other alternative. Then, he quickly rushed to his beloved dear Marion he grabs her as she kisses him on the fore head. Just as the clock struck at midnight, and a new day embarks, Marion gets her powers as a Peace-queen. But alas, it was too late for her now. She tells Marcus that her fate is sealed, she tells him of the prophecy she knows of and tells Marcus about his destiny. With all her powers that she has, and for the sake of her love, she transfers all her powers into Marcus, and transforms him into Sir Marcus, the supreme knight!

But then she gives away too much, and her lifeless body, slowly turns into stone, and flies away as it is converted into dust. Marion becomes an angel, living in the Galdarthian heaven, while Marcus understands his role and gets ready for the life ahead of him. Marcus takes an oath that day that he will never kill another single enemy, for on this day, he killed one, but lost two, both were his near and beloved ones.

The shock of his dead son was too much for the Old supreme knight Rigorad, just before dying, he proclaims his last son, Nortus, as the king of the knights, ruler of Kingslograd and converts him into another supreme knight.

So the only two remaining supreme knights were now Sir Nortus, and Sir Marcus. Nortus being a good friend, forgives Marcus, and proclaims him as his left hand. Both of them ruled the kingdom together. While Marcus used to lead the centurion Battalion, and would hardly use his full strength, as he never wanted to kill anyone, Nortus Never fought any actual

Battle ever! The legend says that he is so strong that he will never meet his match in this universe ever.

So while Nortus was busy governing and ruling Kingslograd, Marcus would fight his battles for him.

It was after some time that I became a ranger knight, and was posted in the centurion battalion, the same which Marcus was leading. We both met and had happy time together. While Marcus was at the top most from the very beginning, I on the other hand slowly getting better and then after some years, I Became an Elite knight, and became second in command, of the Centurion battalion.

"After this, Marcus and I had many adventures together" he said, "we defeated hundreds of monsters, and thousands of Vandals. But it was Marcus who kept his oath, and never killed anyone. And went in countless journeys and battles, without being defeated ever"

I was so engrossed in the story, that I didn't notice that tears were flowing down from my eyes; this story really got me of. I took out my handkerchief and wiped my face it was not totally night, and stars were shining brightly in the sky.

"You really deserve to be called Lucius 'The Story-Teller', it was so wonderful" I said clearing my throat.

"Thank you My Lady, it means a lot to me" he smiled as he said, "You see, that is why My friend has suffered so much pain, and that is why I never bring up this topic when he is nearby"

"I understand," I replied, "it must have been very difficult for him"

Before Lucius could reply someone said from behind, "What will be very difficult for whom?" It was Marcus! I saw that he had found some logs, and also filled up our water bottles! He asked the same question again, but we couldn't let him know. I was almost going to tell him the truth, because he was very persistent, but somehow Lucius got my back.

"Her Majesty was just asking if she is strong enough to defeat four ogres at once, because back on earth she was attacked by them" Lucius said.

Marcus at first saw both of us sharply with his eyes, and then he laughed and said, "she wouldn't have to my friend. Her Guardian, The Headless Horseman will be protect her from any threat!!"

"Exactly," Lucius said looking at me "so you see you are totally safe back on earth as well."

"Yes thank you Marcus" I said as I tried to play my part, "Thank you for the important information"

"My pleasure" he said as he smiled "Now Lucius, have you something to eat, I am famished". Lucius handed him some fruits as Marcus started eating. I saw a reflection of Madhav in him. But mostly I was thinking about Marcus. I never saw anyone like him.

He sacrificed so much and yet he hardly ever complains, he never killed anyone, though he has power to level mountains, he never fell in love again because he had his one true love. How much could a person handle? I had never seen anyone suffering so much yet being so optimistic.

Marcus finished his fruits and said "Now, I will keep the first watch in the night, You Lucius will keep the second one, Ok" he declared.

Soon Marcus was ready to take his first watch, while Lucius was sleeping in his sleeping bag. As I lied down watching Marcus, I knew that something beautiful always happens to good guys like him, and he didn't realized it first but I too was starting to care about him. With this thought, I closed my eyes, put on my bed sheet, and slept peacefully.

Chapter 7

I fight, again, Alone, Again!! With monsters! Again!!!

ave you ever wondered what will happen if you face your biggest fears? Well if a fear of mythical beings can make them crap their pants, then I think you will get the idea or two and you will think twice before facing your fears, something like this happened this day, so here we go.......

When I was sleeping, I had another dream, or vision as what they say. It was such a horrible one; I cannot bear to think about it. In this dream, I was with two other guys, I couldn't see the faces of the other two, but I saw that we all are tied down on the ground, and one thing that was very clear was that it was very hot.

It took me some time to realize that the heat is being increased periodically, and that it is so hot that I can hardly breathe. I then came to an understanding that all of us are in a giant OVEN and we are being baked alive!! It was getting hotter minute by minute, and soon I knew that I won't come out alive.

I tried to get my hands free but in vain, the other guys were unconscious, and I was the only one who could think. I tried to get myself free but I knew that I was losing consciousness, just like my comrades.

Then suddenly I started feeling as if I was on fire, the pain was unbearable, my skin was peeling off! no, not peeling off, it was MELTING!! I WAS BEING MELTED ALIVE!!!

I woke up from my horrible dream, but I didn't see what I expected, there was no one, Lucius, Marcus, Fang, Philip (Lucius's unicorn) weren't there. In fact all there were present were actually me and my unicorn Noel.

She was eating grass while watching me, as if just checking up on me. But this all seemed very weird, I mean, why would those guys who say they are sworn to protect me, would leave me in the morning? This just doesn't seems right.

At first I pinched myself to check whether all of this is a dream or not. But when I was sure that this wasn't a dream, then I started getting worried, I knew that it will be end of mine if another rock giant showed up, so I had to learn where these two knights were, and the most logical solution was, to ask Noel.

"Hey, can I ask you a question?" I asked my pet unicorn, for which she lifted her head, while eating the grass and looked at me as if saying, "Shoot, why not"

"Can you take me to Marcus and Lucius, wherever they might be?" I asked her. I was checking whether she could understand or not, and surprisingly, she did! She stopped eating grass and stomped her hooves on the ground as if indicating, "Hop on"

I sat on her, and then we made our way through the hills. We were inside a place which really resembled a lot like grand canyon. Through the hills and cliffs we marched. And after trotting for at least 5 to 10 minutes we both reached at a spot where the hills were not present, it was covered with green grass, and it was having a pond in between the area.

I was almost lost in my own feelings when I saw Fang, sitting in a very regal manner, as if waiting for his master, and Philip, who was, just as usual eating grass. But this aroused a question in my mind, as to "where are Marcus and Lucius".

Then something caught my eye, I saw that Marcus and Lucius were near the bank of the pond, but they were not wearing their armor jacket. They had nothing apart from their black sleeveless (tank)

They both faced each other, and bowed down. They together lifted their hands and made knuckles, and suddenly Lucius lashed out at Marcus, he ran wildly at towards and then as soon as he reached near him, he tried to punch him, but Marcus blocked it by his hands.

Then Marcus tried to return the favor by a back hand, but Lucius dodged, swirled and landed a strong kick right on Marcus's face. It was just because of his reflexes that in matter of fraction of seconds, Marcus ducked, grabbed Lucius's kick, and tried to give him a slam.

But Lucius wasn't going to give up that easily, his fast movements made Marcus confused and he used his momentum as an advantage, he managed to loosen Marcus's grip on his leg, and right after seeing the opportunity, kicked him right on his chest. Marcus didn't see that one coming, and took the hit, but somehow managed to stay on his feat. Though he was dragged to a little distance by the force of the kick.

Meanwhile Lucius landed safely on his feats, and showed his finger to Marcus as if saying, "Come at me bro". Marcus smiled, and dashed towards his opponent. Lucius to ran towards Marcus and just as they were near, Lucius tried to kick Marcus so that he could fall down, but Marcus's feat weren't on the ground!!

In a matter of seconds, before Lucius realized his mistake, he saw that Marcus had jumped to avoid being hit by the kick, and was ready to punch him. Marcus hit Lucius in midair, and the hit was so strong that Lucius twisted and before he could maintain his balance, Marcus punched him right on his chest. The hit was so strong that Lucius's whole body was lifted and he fell down.

"That is it for today my friend" Marcus said helping his friend he getting up, "better luck next time."

"Well, you know" Lucius said, "at one point in the fight, I had got you"

"For some seconds, yes" Marcus agreed, "I must admit that it looked like you will win this battle, but then, you got overconfident, and that's why you lost the plot"

"I did not!!!" Lucius exclaimed, while wiping his face with a cloth. He gave one to Marcus, and then they both started wearing their arsenal.

"Yes you did" Marcus replied, "I saw it in your eyes"

"OH please spare me the theatricality" Lucius snapped.

"Yes, you were over confident" Marcus kept on accusing.

"No I wasn't" Lucius kept on replying.

"Girls, girls, you both look good" I said so that they could get over the fight, "you both did well, but whatever you did, it was totally cool, what were you doing exactly?"

Both of the knights looked at me together. I could see that they were alarmed to see a third person right behind them, but then things became normal within a second and they both started laughing.

"We were training" Marcus said.

"This was a practice to improve our hand to hand combat style, and both of us didn't wear the helmet or armor, so that we could even the odds" Lucius added.

"Looks pretty intense" I admitted, "hey can you guys teach me some of the moves?"

"Well, mastering this hand to hand combat doesn't happens in one day your majesty" Marcus warned, "you must have commitment."

"In simpler words" Marcus said, "No"

"So you mean you won't teach me?" I asked

"I am sorry, but I don't think that her majesty is the best suited candidate" he replied, "Your hands are weak for this style, and secondly this kind of method of training is strictly restricted for male Knights."

"Is this because I am a girl?" I exclaimed. It reminded me of my parents, who were against me taking Karate lessons from school, just because they thought that I am so fragile, and why did they thought so, because I am a girl.

"Well it can be, because I am not sure whether your body can withstand the punches, and that is without your armor-jacket" he replied. I was astonished by his reply, I mean, this was the coolest way of self defense I have ever seen and I won't be able to learn it just because I am a girl, I could take on a full sized ORC for god's sake! I had to teach the knight a lesson. (I must have been out of my mind, right?)

"Well, let's make a deal" I declared, "we both will fight, and if I manage to land even a single punch or kick on your body, you will have to teach me, if I couldn't do it, then we will have it your way, deal?" (I was really out of my mind, though I just checked if the fighting style was any good, but this! I really surprised myself that day)

Marcus first looked at Lucius, then smiled and said, "well, to even the odds, my queen, you can wear your helmet, and your jacket, but to protect myself, you must allow me to wear my jacket, so that we can have a fair battle"

Lucius tried reasoning with him, but Marcus knew that he was in for some fun that morning, but the worst part was, Lucius wasn't reasoning with Marcus to protect himself from me, he was trying to tell him to go easy with me; he was protecting me from him!

I took on Lunar Ray; it quickly transformed into my helmet, and wore my jacket, while Marcus was only fighting with his armor-jacket.

"So my lady, what shall be the time limit?" He asked me as he got ready for the fight.

"The limit is when I give up" I replied trying to sound cool.

"Splendid!!" Marcus said.

I made a simple boxing posture that came into my mind. Marcus was just standing a few feats away from me, he had hands on his back, and he was just looking at me, calmly.

I ran towards him and punched at him right on the first chance I had got, but, he quickly dodged it!!!! And instead, my punch got hit by the ground, and crushed it making a medium sized hole, with cracks and small crevices. I tried to punch him again, but then he blocked it!

My punch could make a 20 foot Orc fly in the air but Marcus blocked it as if he was blocking a punch of a five year old girl! And he smiled! I mean, was he even trying to fight?

This made me even angrier, I rapidly started punching Marcus, but he would dodge them, deflect them, or block them, and he even yawned in between, as if he was getting bored!! It was about time I learned that I bit more than I could chew.

After some six-seven minutes, when I was completely drained, I admitted my defeat. I was panting, though I couldn't manage to land even a single punch on Marcus, my main purpose was successful, to check whether this art of fighting was any good?

Marcus on the other hand, didn't even break a sweat, and he was smiling or yawning all the time!

"I am the supreme knight your majesty" he said, "I have lead hundreds of missions to success, surely I could manage to deflect your every attack"

"But, how did you do it?" I asked, "My punch was strong enough that a full sized Orc couldn't withstand it, then how did you deflected it with such ease?" yes, I am serious; he really did to it with great ease.

"Having strength doesn't always mean that you are powerful" he replied, "your real strength comes from your heart, and it is known as will power. The will to take action, and the will to stop an attack, this is a unique power that may take many years to strengthen, but if you master your will, then you master your life"

"And what does that mean?" I asked wiping my face with my handkerchief. Both of the knights looked at each other, and I realized what a fool I made of myself in front of them.

"I understand that you are desperate to learn this fighting style, but you must prove your worth, my queen" Lucius interrupted in between.

"After all, only the elite and supreme knight are strong enough to master this art of fighting" Marcus chimed in. And I rolled my eyes.

But then, Marcus's smile faded as he cried, "Oh my god, we have wasted so much time, we have to make haste." And we all got on our animals. And I knew what a grave mistake I made.

After this incident, we all were trotting on the back of our animals. We had left Derekus hills, and we were galloping in the 'Sander lands of North.'

We rode all the day on the back of our animals. Morning, then afternoon, then evening. These three phases of our day were almost over.

It was near dusk and we still hadn't found anyplace where we will spend our night. I was riding for so long that my back was aching.

Why wouldn't Marcus stop, if he knows that I do not have much experience riding on horses, let alone unicorns, (though the only remarkable difference between those two is the presence of horns)

"Why the hell Marcus isn't stopping for one minute" I asked Lucius. And do you know, we were having this conversation while riding on our unicorns, who at the current moment were galloping through the grasslands.

"I don't know" He replied stupidly, "Maybe because we wasted a lot of time in the morning for someone who wanted to have a fight with one of the most legendary warriors the universe has ever seen?"

"What" I looked at him, "what do you mean? I was just checking how good are you guys without your arsenal"

"Very poor way to check our potential" he replied. And looked at me, as if saying, "you know what to do"

"Alright, alright," I confessed, "I am going to him, and I will apologize".

When I said this, then Lucius flashed a smile of victory. He was really good in his way. I made my way past him, and reached near Fang. Marcus was looking forward, and paid no attention to me.

He was really mad because I wasted so much time in the morning for my stupid desire to prove that I am a good fighter.

"Hey" I sad, as Noel dashed near Fang, "I am sorry for what happened in the morning, I really messed up."

"The fault is not yours My lady," He said, "You were just quenching the thirst of your curiosity, I was the one to protect you, I was the one who should have been responsible, I should have checked the time."

"But I acted immaturely" I said, "I should have been more serious about how much important this is for your world, I am sorry"

"You did nothing to ask for an apology my queen, but in the future just remind me about my duty, if I don't take things as seriously as they should." he said. This guy was not only amazing, but nice hearted also. We all knew that it was my entire fault, but still he didn't complain. 'I am going to make up to him' I thought.

We reached the Ginger woods by nightfall, and it took almost half an hour more to reach at a place that was nice for making beds. Lucius collected firewood, and had got some fruits from the forest. This forest was just like the 'Beatle wood' but the only difference was that here the trees were not very straight, they were not very tall, at max they could reach 50 feet. It was like a jungle you can find back on earth, and yes, there was a smell of ginger-breads in the jungle. According to Lucius, this smell never stopped.

I was reading my Archie comic while Marcus and Lucius were busy in un packing their beds. It was totally dark. Both of them took out their armor jackets.

Marcus and Lucius were quite hungry, while I wasn't, so they took a bite of their fruits, (which actually was a very bad idea). As they took the piece of their guava in their mouth, they spit it out! I mean literally, they spit it out as if the guava had a cyanide pill in it.

"What happened to you guys!" I exclaimed.

"I am sorry for the behavior My liege, but I have never eaten any fruit with such a bad taste!" Marcus said.

"This isn't natural" Lucius added, "Most of the fruits coming in Kingslograd are supplied by this forest, and never before had there been such a repulsive taste of any fruit, which grew up here"

"So what does this have to do with anything?" I asked rolling my eyes.

Marcus then added, "why waste time in simple fruits, when our majesty has prepared our food" (it is like a rhyme, right?)

"But I thought that you both didn't like my home made sandwiches" I said slyly, what, you don't expect me to take revenge?

"No, it is not that, we never hated you food my lady, but we just are not accustomed to eat new things, to acquire new taste, that's why we had to reject it" Lucius replied.

"Then why eat it now?" I asked trying to make them wish that they shouldn't have rejected my recipe.

"Because we have no other alternative" Marcus said. This time, he was serious, and even I felt that I have gone too far. Both of them had saved my life more than once, so I can help them now. I gave them my sand-which. They both ate it, without making any face but then I knew that they didn't like it.

Both of them had two sandwiches each. And now my stock was a little low, I had only two lunch boxes left, for a journey which was still at the minimum two to three days long.

After eating my sandwich, both of them were content. Marcus Looked at me and said, "Thank you my queen, for the favor, now I shall show you something very beautiful in return"

"What are you planning to show me?" I asked smiling.

"Come with me" Marcus replied "Lucius, take care of the camp till we return", and we both started walking towards in the jungle. We walked and we walked till we were near a place which was not covered in thick bushes or trees. But then Marcus closed my eyes gently with his hands.

He said "This is a surprise, you have to wait for sometime". I was growing impatient by the minute. Then Marcus took me in a place where I couldn't feel any tree or bush or anything apart from his hands, and the grass beneath my sneakers.

"Look upwards" He said as he removed his hands from my eyes. I did as he told me, and I am happy that I listened to him. I saw a sky full of stars, and not just stars, it was as if I am watching the whole galaxy in high-definition. It was one of the most beautiful scenes I ever saw in my life.

"Beautiful, isn't it" Marcus said.

"Yes, really very beautiful" I replied still gazing at the stars.

"Marion loved to watch stars like this" he replied, and then I realized that he knew what Lucius and I talked about the other night.

"Do not think me as a fool, my queen" Marcus said, as he smiled, "Lucius did tell you that Fang tells me everything when I am not present, well Fang being a wolf has extremely sensitive ears, and he heard everything that you both said last night"

We both looked at each other, and then burst out Laughing! Really, we were laughing just like two kindergarten students. We had a really good time, watching the beautiful scenery,

But then suddenly Marcus placed his hands on my lips, and instructed me to keep quiet.

"what happened?" I whispered

"I think I just heard something" He replied, he was going to take out his knight specs when he shouted, "Curses! I forgot my arsenal back at the camp!"

Then suddenly the bush in front of him started shaking wildly, and I knew nothing good comes from a bush that shakes wildly, but then, it came out to be that it was Lucius.

At first, I took a sigh of relief, but after watching his face, I knew something was going on. He was panting, and he was not wearing his knight arsenal. It was as if he was running from something. I went towards him with Marcus.

"What happened my friend?" Marcus asked him.

"They came from everywhere, I didn't have a chance to strike back, and they took away my arsenal, as well as yours" he replied panting half the time.

"Who took our arsenal away?" Marcus demanded

"I have no time to answer Marcus, you should run, I can hold them, but I don't know without my arsenal, for how much time can I tackle them." Lucius instructed.

"But who is attacking us?" Marcus cried.

"Goblins Marcus, GOBLINS!" shouted Lucius as the sky was covered with hairy human-ish kind of guys with bat like wings!!!

The sky was filled with menacing laughter as if possessed clowns are laughing (just like you see in horror films). As they came near, flying towards us, I noticed that they were wearing nothing apart from a simple piece of skin covering their private parts.

They had big white eyes, pure white. Their face was covered in wrinkles, they had very thin lips, and very big teeth. They had really sharp fingernails, and pointy fingers. And they had talons for their feat. They were having really long and pointy ears, and one more thing, they were green in color!

"Run!" Lucius shouted, "RUN!!!" and both of us ran as fast as we could, but Marcus stood behind. For a moment there, I thought that he will fight the goblins, just like he was doing when we clashed with the rock giant.

But then, Lucius looked back and cried, "Oh no, I have to save him! How could I be so careless!" then he looked at me and said, "My Queen, don't come with me, run, as fast as your legs can take you, RUN, AND DON'T LOOK BACK. RUN!!"

And at this first sign, I started running as fast as I could. I knew that the goblins were closing. As I glanced back, I saw that Lucius is helping Marcus to make a run for it. I saw that Marcus wasn't actually there to fight the goblins.

He was standing there because he was so scared that he was almost paralyzed. Lucius was helping him in running, as I saw his face, I saw that Marcus was so scared that he could hardly leave an expression.

'He was scared to death! A guy who could lift mountains was scared to death by puny flying people, how weirder can this place be?' I thought, and the thought was bad. They both weren't fast enough. The goblins got to them. Though Lucius managed to knock out the first 4 to 5 goblins easily, but they were just too much for him to handle. The goblins surrounded them, and took both of them. As for me, I was not stopping, but my legs were now hurting. I was running continuously for ten minutes. I finally stopped when I was exhausted. I glanced back, and saw no one. I gave a sigh of relief, but as I walked forward, a goblin jumped right in front of me.

He was not very tall. Actually, he was smaller than me by a couple of inches. He had a very menacing look. He saw me, and started checking me with bulging out eyes. He then said, "Food, I eat food, you"

I somehow misunderstood him and said, "food, yes, very tasty, you a vegetarian?" this was the best I could think at that moment, to buy myself some time.

He said again, "NO, you food, YOU FOOD, I eat YOU!"

"Ok," I said trying to control my breath, and trying to remain calm and I started moving backwards, "You elevated fast, but you see, I am not very tasty" I licked my hand, and made a very terrible gesture, and said, "Me, very bad taste, me very bad taste"

But he replied "No, you good smell, you taste good. I eat you now!!! I HUNGRY I EAT YOU!!!!"

I tried to run, but he was way too fast for me. But then, I realized that I could try to fight him I mean Lucius kicked butts of like five to six goblins without his helmet, so why can't I.

I turned back, and slapped him as hard as I could. The goblins took the hit, and fell down. For a moment, I was pretty happy with myself. There were some monsters in this world that were not that strong.

But then he stood up, and roared at me!! He jumped right on top of me, and caught me off guard. He was hitting me just like a small child. But he was way too strong for a small child. I underestimated him greatly. He was even stronger than me! At that moment, I once again felt that this will be the last time when I open my eyes, because he will kill me, and eat me!

But boy, this time as well, I was wrong again!

Just as I thought that this will be the end of me, I heard the sound of hooves galloping towards me. At first, I thought that the headless horseman was coming once again, but this time, as I opened my eyes to see who it was, I saw that it was Noel! She charged with all her speed towards the goblin.

Before the goblin realized what was going on, Noel stabbed her horn in his chest. But the goblin was still not dead, he was hitting Noel with everything he had got. But then noel didn't stop at there. She galloped taking the goblin with her, and hit a tree. The impact practically impaled the goblin, and he could not bear the pain. He started transforming into a rock, and then flew away by becoming dust.

"GOOD GIRL!! Thank you so much" I cried as I hugged her. She saved my life. And that too when I was most desperate!

She looked at me, and grunted, as if saying, "No big deal, just don't push it, alright. I won't save your butt every-time"

I still smiled at her. It was the first time, I thought any good thing about an animal. The goblin could have killed Noel, with his blows, but this didn't stop her, she risked her life saving me.

Then it hit me, 'What about Marcus and Lucius?' I thought to myself. I asked Noel that where could they be. She stood up and instructed me to hop on.

The place was far, and the ride was very cranky. My back started hurting again. But then after a couple of hours I got down from Noel as we reached near the place. I started searching what was going on, so I hid behind a big bush, while I instructed Noel to lay low. As I started observing what was going on, I couldn't believe my eyes.

There were almost hundreds, and hundreds of goblins, some small some big, some even very large (like seven foot tall and bulky large). It was a whole community of goblins. They had tents, big tables to eat on, and huge bon fires.

It was not very good-looking, I saw that Fang was trapped in a wooden cage. He was barking and growling at every goblin who passed, but no one paid attention to him, some were even teasing him. Near Fang was Philip, the unicorn. His rope was tightly knotted with a big wooden nail in the ground. And he was lying on the ground as his legs were bind together.

Then, as I looked further, I saw that there was a huge black vessel, like a cauldron of a witch. The goblins were placing vegetables and salt in it, as if preparing a dish.

Near the cauldron, I saw the skeletons of humans, and a whole pile of them! I soon realized that the goblins had captured us, not for a bounty, but because they wanted to eat us! We were their food. The goblins were cannibals!! It was just like my dream, but instead of a huge microwave or oven, it was a cauldron.

I looked further, and soon, I found out where both of the knights were taken. Both of them were standing near a vertical log. Their hands, and legs were strapped behind it, and they were not having their helmet, or their jacket. Lucius was very uncomfortable, he was desperately trying to get himself free. He was nagging, he was twisting, but all in vain. While Marcus could Hardly do anything! It was as if he had got a shock!! Whenever any goblin would come near him, he would cry and shout saying "Get away you monster, let me be! Don't kill me, I beg of you!! BEGONE!!" he was scared to death, as if he saw a ghost. He was so scared that I felt as if he had a so called *'GOBLINOPHOBIA' (no, I made that up)*

But, I knew that I couldn't waste any time in watching a grown superhero cry like a kid, I had to find their arsenal. I looked everywhere I could, but I still couldn't find their arsenal anywhere. I was just lucky to be wearing my armor jacket, but as for my helmet, I had no idea where Lunar ray was.

When I was almost about to lose hope, I saw a goblin nearby playing with silver colored specs. For a while, I was confused what to do, but then, I realized that he was playing with Lunar Ray! The goblin was playing with My helmet!

I whistled him, and he noticed me. At first I was dead scared, I thought that he will shout and inform everyone. But then, I tried to make him calm, by putting my fingers on my lips. He understood at first! (OH thank god!) and instructed him to come near. He did, and then, I tried to snatch Lunar ray from him.

But his grip was too tight. Just as I tried to take Lunar ray from him, he growled at me, and kept it with him. Then, I got an idea.

I called him again, and said "You want to keep the helmet". He looked at the specs, and nodded.

I took out my MP3 player, and said, "You don't want this?". His eyes got fixed at the MP3 player. I turned it on, and gave it to him. He got lost in the lights of my player. His grip loosened, and I got my chance.

I quickly snatched my Lunar Ray at the right opportunity, but things got pretty ugly. He became angry, and shouted at the top of his voice.

This attracted the attention of every goblin, knight unicorn, and giant wolf, and what-not, right at us. And the only thought I had in my mind was 'Oh crap'.

All the goblins together roared, and dashed towards me, and the goblin that had my MP3, got so angry, that he crushed it to pieces! And this made me angry too, because my parents had promised not to give me another MP3 player till I decide to take a good subject in 11th.

I quickly wore Lunar ray. It was just at the right time, as the goblin jumped at me to hit me. I punched him so hard that he went flying away and fell somewhere dozen of yards away. The goblins quickly started attacking me, I had little time to react because they were damn fast. And during the fight, my visor was showing me the information of the goblins, which was somewhat, like this:

SPECIES:GOBLINS

HOMEPLACE: GOBLINAGARD ISLE.

STRENGTH: UNDEFYING SPEED AND AGILITY. ABILITY TO FLY, AND FAST REFLEXES.

WEAKNESS: SUNLIGHT.

What did it meant by saying "weakness is sunlight"? I couldn't understand, but as the visor was cleared, I got ready to fight. As a goblin dashed towards me, I hit him so hard that, well, oh you get the idea.

It was practically one against one hundred. I didn't know for how long could I keep up? I was hitting every goblin I could lay my hands on. I was not letting them come near me. Because it could prove to be dangerous!!

I somehow managed to tackle them to even the odds. They were now almost half of them.

"What" I shouted, trying to make myself look tough, "Is that all you've got!"

And, yes, that was a very, very bad idea. Initially, all the goblins laughed, one of them took out a huge war-horn, and blew it. Within seconds after blowing it, I started hearing flaps of batwings from throughout the forest.

And in no time, the sky was totally covered with an entire army of Goblins!! The visor showed:

GOBLINS IN PURSUIT: 500

I could not understand what to do. I ran towards Lucius to ask him, and cleared my way by hitting every goblin who was trying to stop me.

"Hey Lucius!" I said as I punched a goblin who was trying to hit me, "What the hell should I do now!"

"I am happy that you could make it!" Lucius said.

"Yeah, I owed you one" I replied, and then I shouted, "HEY, NO BITING!!" I kicked a goblin who was trying to bite my leg, "where is your arsenal?" I asked.

"It is over there" he said, pointing by his eyes, towards a goblin tent nearby, "this is where they had our tools,"

The army was closing in.

"Hey," I said as I blocked an attack of a goblin, "I won't be OFFENDED by a few suggestions you know! What do you mean by 'weakness of goblins is sunlight?'"

"Oh that" he said cheerfully "all you have to do is to tackle with them till the dawn, and just as the first light of sun touches the surface of this forest, the goblins will be turned to ashes". He had some guts to stay so cheerful, if I had it my way, I could eat him up!!

"What are you---" I didn't even got the chance to finish my sentence, a large seven foot tall goblin grabbed me by my leg, and started slamming me over 6 times right on the ground, as if he was slamming a teddy bear!

"Oh you've got to be KIDDING me!!" I shouted. I ran towards the big goblin, grabbed him by his head, and gave him a strong slam. My slam was strong enough to break the ground beneath the body of the goblin.

And just in time, when over 500 goblins saw me hitting another goblin. All I could do was to give a stupid smile and say, "I don't think that we can talk out about this, can we?" and the army of goblin waged a war against me!!

I was trying my best to keep them at bay by punching them, kicking them, or slamming them. I was doing my best, but I was getting exhausted slowly.

"Hey Lucius!" I cried out for him, he was busy trying to get free, while Marcus was so shacked that he was knocked unconscious.

"Yes My Lady!" he shouted.

"How much time till sunrise?" I asked.

He thought for it for some seconds, then said, "it will take at least 2-3 hours from now." And I felt that this is how my end will come. But thanks to Noel, who was watching everything, gave me a helping hand.

She started hitting the goblins, to distract their attention from me. She succeeded, and I got the chance to help Marcus and Lucius. But before I could reach there to help them, Lucius stopped me, and said, "My queen, though your intentions are true, it will mean the end of us. The goblins will make sure to kill us before we reach near the tent where our tools are kept. Free the animals first. They will help you in this battle"

"You think that this is easy! I am so tired right now." I shouted.

"Well," he replied, "as a matter of fact I think it is easy, I mean, they are goblins, any knight can handle them, they are the most primitive monster force in Galdarth,"

"Well, it could have been easy for me, if someone wouldn't be too cocky on teaching m a few moves so that I could help myself" I snapped back.

"My queen," Lucius said, "YOU REALLY have a very bad timing! Just free the animals, they will help you!"

I nodded, and dashed to help Philip. With one pull, I broke the ropes, and freed him. He, just like Noel, started hitting the goblins. Next, I helped, to free fang. I broke his cage, and Fang jumped out and gave a deafening roar, and pounced at the goblins.

"Now this is what I call reinforcement!" I said and I started fighting alongside the animals. Even though the fight was pretty even, those 2 hours were very difficult for me to handle. I was hitting them with everything I had, yet it was like they just kept coming.

But soon, as the ray of sunlight fell on Galdarth, the goblins started panicking. Everyone was trying run away, and find a shelter, but just as the light fall on land, The monsters let out a cry, and were turned to stone, and then soon into dust. Marcus and Lucius were freed, and their arsenal was given back, but actually, it was only Lucius, Marcus was deep asleep, it must have been by the fear of the goblins.

I was so exhausted that I nearly fell down after the battle, but Lucius helped me in standing me up, "You did a great job My Lady" he said, "we will forever be in your debt"

"No I owed you both a ton," I said, "but, if you want to help me, then please, give me some hours to sleep, I am very tired, and sleepy." Just as when I said this. Marcus got up and gave a big yawn. He had a big and cheerful smile on his face.

"Ah so you both are awake" he said, "So I don't think we should waste anymore time, shall we push on and head for the new destination?" and as he said this, I felt like strangling him, and the only thought that I had in my mind was, 'Marcus, you are not serious'.

Chapter 8

We spend the night in a Fairy-Tale town

Well, after last night battle, the afterhours were pretty decent, but even though I am dying to tell you the end of the story, I don't want to destroy your suspense, so..........

"Marcus, you are not serious!" I cried, "I was up all night trying to save both of your scared butts, and when I do, then you don't remember what happened last night, do you?"

Marcus tried to think but, all he could remember was having my homemade sandwiches. Well, this wasn't unexpected, what would you do if you were up against your greatest fear, either you' run and hide, or die trying to fight it. Marcus couldn't do either of these. So, it was sort of normal to suffer from amnesia. But what about me! I am far away from my home, and my dimension, so if I can take on all of this, then so should he.

"Forget it!" I exclaimed "I literally need some rest, I will not walk even a foot further, until I get some sleep!"

"But, your majesty" Marcus pleaded, "Time is of the essence"

"I don't care what will happen to the universe, I need to get some sleep, got it, and I want it now!" I snapped, sometimes, I amaze even myself.

Lucius, whispered something in Marcus's ears. They both whispered something very secretly, and then Marcus turned to me for the conclusion.

"My queen" He said, "I am in your debt, you saved both of us from the goblins, but as we waste each second, and the lesser hope will be left to save our dimensions. Though we will not snatch your 'right to sleep' we too need to make up for the lost time"

"So, where are you getting?" I asked.

"Your majesty can have her sleep, but on Fang, we will keep moving, but so slow that you shall not be disturbed, while I shall mount on Noel, for your convenience." and now I was confirmed that I won't get a minute rest, because I need pure silence to sleep, and my bed should not move, which is not possible when you are sleeping on Fang.

I didn't argue after that, it was my entire fault that we had to make up for the lost time, so I agreed. The knights packed their sacs, and got ready for the journey ahead. Only I was the one who yawned and was thinking how to get some sleep on a giant wolf.

As I mounted up on him, I felt so comfortable. His fur was very soft, and it felt as if I am leaning on a pillow. This time, Marcus didn't went on galloping with his animals, but we started off by walking. I leaned my head against him, and as I closed my eyes, I started sleeping heavily. And I seriously mean sleeping.

But this time, I didn't have a dream, or vision, it was just plain normal sleep. The next time I opened my eyes, I saw that I was still on the giant wolf, Marcus and Lucius smiled as I opened my eyes. The thing was that Even though Fang was walking, I slept like a baby in a cradle.

"For how long was I sleeping?" I asked them.

"Well," Lucius said scratching his head, "noon has passed, and so, you must be sleeping for at least 8 hours"

I sat up, and splashed some water on my face. "So, have we covered any distance?" I asked,

"We did cover 7 Zilos, My queen" He replied.

"And what does that mean?"

"Almost 35 to 40 kilometers" He replied.

Marcus tried to cut in by saying, "If it is not much trouble my queen, can I get back on Fang?". I quickly got down the big wolf, and got on Noel.

"So, did you miss me?" I asked her, as she whipped me with her hairy tail.

"Yeah, I know, I missed you too" I replied, and she grunted as if saying, "yeah, whatever"

Then, as Marcus hoisted himself on Fang, we started increasing our speed. For the rest of the day we were on our animals, and we didn't stop for anything.

From noon, to afternoon, to evening, till nightfall, we were riding on our animals. Soon just as the sun was about to set. In front of us was a sign, Marcus, saw the sign and read it aloud "𝔚𝔢𝔩𝔠𝔬𝔪𝔢 𝔱𝔬 𝔇𝔯𝔞𝔰𝔱𝔬𝔫 𝔙𝔦𝔩𝔩𝔞𝔤𝔢"

"Yes, this is it" Marcus told Lucius, "We shall find an INN and spend the night there, have you the rubies?"

"Yes, I have them" Lucius replied taking out a handful of rubies and jewels from one of his sac. Marcus noticed and we made our way in the city.

"My queen" Lucius said, "Do you believe in fairy-tales?"

"Seriously!" I said rolling my eyes, "you are asking someone who has seen ogres, knights, werewolves, Orcs and what-not?"

"No, I mean the fairy-tales of your world" he asked.

"Actually, at the moment, I think if I said no, then I am going to be wrong, right?" I replied. I knew that something was up to his sleeves. Or else he wouldn't have asked me this question.

"Well, if you do, then I am sure that you will like this Place" He said. And yes, he was right once again. As we entered the village, I thought that I have entered in Disney-land, just without the rides and stalls and stuffs.

The place was full of small and beautiful houses made from wood. We were on a street which was made from bricks, and the street lamps were not made from electric light but from oil lamps, having a candle in it. The houses were having very cheerful colors, such as yellow, white, and even pink! Almost every building was having a chimney. The houses were having big windows from where I could see that families were eating their food on the table together.

The streets were full of people, who were walking with a purpose, they would turn and greet me saying "How do you do?" or "welcome to Draston my lovely"

The men were wearing baggy pants, (which by the way, were not even near pants) it was more like a baggy lower, and they were wearing shirts which were bigger than there upper body. Some were also wearing a three piece suit, but their shirts and trousers were very baggy, and some were even wearing big Lincoln Hats.

The ladies were wearing a robe that I didn't recognize, maybe because it was considered historic in my world. They were mostly wearing a gown, which was then made fit for the figure of the wearing women by the help of some ribbons. Some were wearing colorful frocks, and some were wearing big skirts with dull colored tops.

Instead of roads, there were streets, made up of bricks. The town was filled with small canals. Which were up to 7 feet wide. There were small bridges made up of bricks and wood, we crossed it.

As we moved on, I saw many different kinds of buildings, some saying '𝕷𝕚𝕓𝕣𝕒𝕣𝕪' some saying '𝕿𝕠𝖜𝕟 𝕳𝕠𝖘𝖕𝕚𝖙𝕒𝖑' some saying '𝕴𝕟𝕟'. I saw that there was a 20 foot tall statue of a knight. He was wearing a cape as well, but his helmet was a little different.

His helmet had a holder in the middle top part, from where long spiky thin hairs were attached, like a Spartan. His one hand was pointing towards east and other was at the back. And the rest was almost same.

"Hey Lucius?" I called him, "For whom is this statue built?"

"That my lady," He replied, "is Zarthur, the first supreme knight ever, this statue was made to remind the Galdarthians of his vision"

Before I could ask another question, Marcus told us to stop. We were near a stable so he said, "We must our leave animals, at the stable your majesty, the guard will make sure that your unicorns are well fed, and well cared." I and Lucius did what he told us, while he got down from Fang and ordered him to roam free in the jungle. But before going, he took his arsenal with him.

"What about Fang, who will take care of him?" I asked.

"Fang can take care of himself, besides, he hasn't eaten anything for 4 days, He should go out for his hunt, before the town folk ask for a missing pet" he said and laughed, "I think you should take your arsenal as well Lucius" He told him, "And you too my lady." And I did as he told me. Then as we made our way to the stable as Fang made his way for the forest.

In the stable, there were not only horses, but other unicorns too, and of different colors and sizes. There were even Pegasus! (you know those horses with wings and can fly). There were also 5 foot tall eagles walking on four limbs and were having big wings!

After giving the unicorns to the stable-man, we then went to an inn nearby. it was getting cooler by every minute, and the streets were emptying too.

"You wouldn't like staying outside in this place at night your majesty," Lucius whispered, "It gets dead cold out here, it even snows sometimes, but then, we have only one night to spend here."

This made me shiver, and I started feeling cold. But soon we came across an inn named, "𝕾𝔦𝔢𝔤𝔣𝔯𝔦𝔢𝔡'𝔰 𝕴𝔫𝔫. 𝕽𝔬𝔬𝔪𝔰 𝔞𝔳𝔞𝔦𝔩𝔞𝔟𝔩𝔢 𝔞𝔰 𝔴𝔢𝔩𝔩" Marcus opened the door, and as I entered, I started feeling warm. The place had a look like a 500 year old bar. Almost everything was made from wood.

It was having wooden circular tables, with wooden benches. The ordering table was long and rectangular. There were three large metal chandeliers hanging from the ceiling. Each big enough to hold twenty candles. There was a fire place. the wooden floor creaked as I moved.

The people there were busy in their own business. Some were playing chess, some were playing cards, some were sitting near the fire place and chatting, some were old friends who were gathered around a table and were singing a folk song in a language which I could not understand, while drinking big mugs of beer, while some were love-birds who were enjoying each other's company and their fine wine.

Marcus and Lucius sat on the ordering table and asked for the bartender. The bartender was a big man, at least 6 feet tall, and was wearing a big baggy (AGAIN!!) three piece suit, but just by looking at it, I could tell that the quality wasn't very good. The man was very fat and bulky. He was bald, but his head was hidden because of his hat. He had big moustache. It was butterfly maybe (it is a style of moustache, Idiot!). he came near us while wiping a big beer mug.

And as he saw the knights, he at first was startled. And both of the knights smiled at him.

"Marcus, here at my inn!" He said happily, "And You have brought Lucius too, oh it should be a good day, how many years has it been, one, two?"

"Two years, three months, four weeks and five days" Lucius corrected him.

"AHA" He replied happily, "Witty Lucius, you didn't lose your sense of humor, did you, I see not! And Marcus, how are you, last time you both met me was on the battlefield of Gondar, I was the battalion's chef remember?"

"Yes, I remember you Siegfried!" Marcus said smiling, "How could I forget the delicious meals that you cooked for the knights. I would survive each day just to eat your cooked food!"

And after a couple of seconds, all the three of them hugged each other, as if there was an old family reunion. They all laughed for some times sharing old jokes, and then the man said, "Alright, this moment deserves a celebration, let me bring my best quality beer, and let us enjoy the rest of the night, shall we!"

"As much as I hate to say this," Marcus replied, "we are here for the order, our mission is to escort her majesty to her throne, to well, you know protect the world and all that sort of stuff, but this time, if we fail, almost all the existence of any being will be wiped out."

"So, do you mean" the bartender asked looking at me.

"Yes," Replied Marcus.

"So it means that the prophecy is true?"

"Yes"

"Is she from earth?"

"Yes!"

"So, she will be taking her throne?"

"YES!"

"Does that mean--" he was going to say something but Marcus cut him in between saying, "Yes, and probably, the answer to the next question, is also YES"

Then he quickly turned to me, and shake my hands, and said, "well bless my soul, if I aren't lucky to have you in my Inn, I am Siegfried my queen, at your service."

"We need your help my friend" Lucius asked, "we need a place to spend the night, so we thought, you may help us."

"I will help you in any way you can" He replied, and gave me a key from his drawer, "This my queen is the royal suite, you can spend the night there"

"And we'd like two common rooms please" Marcus said.

"No friend of mine sleeps in a common room," he exclaimed. "you both can sleep in the private suite. Each suite for all of you"

"Thank you Siegfried" Lucius said, and Marcus added, "You are a true friend."

But Siegfried answered, "No, we all should thank you to undertake this immense responsibility." He then cupped his hands in front of his mouth and shouted, "For the return of my friends tonight, FREE BEER TO EVERYONE IN THIS INN!" and everyone started hooting happily.

I felt a little uncomfortable. The place was almost stinking with an alcoholic tinge. But, somehow I kept my nose shut, and breathed from my mouth in such a way so that no one could notice me.

Siegfried took a small chandelier, and we all followed him to a dark hall. He took us near the staircase, gave us our keys and called out "OH Jocelyn!!" and as he said this, a blonde and tall girl appeared from the darkness. She had hair which were so long that they were till her knees, and she had pretty green eyes, her face was filled with mud and sweat, which proved that she was working all the day.

"Yes Father?" she replied.

"Meet Marcus and Lucius, they are the knights of the order" said Siegfried, "They are here to spend a night here. They have brought a special guest as well. Will you help them to their specific chambers, can you do it my darling? Here are the keys, and here is the chandelier"

"Certainly father" she said, then she turned to us and said "Now guest, please follow me."

We all went with her, and Siegfried went back saying "Goodnight knights! Sleep tight, don't let the monsters bite!" (This hardly made any sense)

We crossed the first floor, and went through the hallway. It was so dark that I could hardly see anything, and even with the chandelier, I could not see even four feet away. Jocelyn opened one door, and said "first Private suite for Lucius" and Lucius went in. Then came the second suite and she said "private suite registered for Sir Marcus" and Marcus went in. Then lastly came a door which was at the end of the hallway, and she said "Royal suite registered for Nikita" and I went in the room.

The first thought that came in my mind was 'GEE, do they even understand the meaning of the word 'Suit'?' the room had a couple of chandeliers on the wall, with burning candles on it, a bigger chandelier was hanging from the ceiling.

It was big enough for handling 20 candles. The room was well alight, but that is the only good thing. It had a bed, a wooden table with one small chair, a drawer, with a mirror upon it, and a fire place.

"This is our best room" she said.

"Hate to see the worst" I murmured.

"I beg your pardon?"

"Oh, no, nothing, I just said 'I hate to sleep in the worst"

"Oh, ok, enjoy your stay here Nikita" she said and closed the door.

Just as she said this, I got surprised, 'How did she came to know my name?' I thought. Because no one knew my name apart from Lucius and Marcus, and she said it twice since we met. I thought about it for some minutes, but then left the topic, maybe because as everyone was aware of the prophecy, they could be aware of the name of the person too.

I tried to find a toilet in the room, but all I could find was a room with a sink, and a bucket. After watching that, I questioned my own stomach whether I should go for the call of nature or not, 'well, extreme circumstances require extreme measures' I thought.

After getting free from my toilet problem I brushed my teeth, changed my clothes, and entered in my room.

As I came back, I saw that someone had placed a metallic utensil on my bed. It was with a note saying "𝔓𝔬𝔯𝔯𝔦𝔡𝔤𝔢 𝔴𝔦𝔱𝔥 𝔰𝔬𝔪𝔢 𝔡𝔯𝔶 𝔣𝔯𝔲𝔦𝔱𝔰. 𝔒𝔲𝔯 𝔠𝔬𝔪𝔭𝔩𝔦𝔪𝔢𝔫𝔱𝔰. 𝔈𝔫𝔧𝔬𝔶 𝔶𝔬𝔲𝔯 𝔰𝔱𝔞𝔶"

I took my spoon and started eating my porridge. It was so sweet and tasty that before I could realize it, it was finished. I lay down on my bed for a while, and tried to sleep, but I couldn't as I had slept in the morning.

I tried to find my Mp3 player, but then remembered that I had sacrificed it for my knight arsenal while fighting with the goblins. I tried to read my comic, but then I wasn't really feeling to read. It was all too boring to do anything.

So I put on my knight jacket, and placed Lunar ray in my pocket for protection, and decided to go to Marcus and Lucius and ask their permission to roam in this town. I was just about to open my door, when I heard a knock.

I jumped back in my bed and covered myself from the bed sheet to prevent anybody from seeing my armor (this was the most logical thought at the moment.)

"Come in" I said.

"I apologize to bother you Nikita" said Jocelyn as she entered. Her robes were not the same, earlier, she was wearing a black dress now, and her hair were now open, "But I am your companion for the night"

"Meaning?" I said raising my eyebrows. I mean, why would I need a 'companion' to sleep. This was really weird and awkward.

"My father said that if you are not able to sleep, then I shall help you in your sleep" she replied.

Though I could not understand a word she said, I invited her in my room, and asked her "Tell me Jocelyn, how you knew my name?

She was getting stressed at this one question "I don't know what you mean, My father already told me your name"

"Really, I didn't see him do so" I replied casually.

But before either of us could say anything, Siegfried shouted from the ground floor, "Jocelyn, where are you honey! Come down please, don't disturb them!"

"You said that your father sent you here" I asked, "then why doesn't he know where you are, and why is he calling you?" I was getting suspicious about the loyalty of this girl. With each question, she would get angrier.

But what actually got my attention was her long hair were becoming shorter by itself! No scissor, no razor, nothing. And upon that it was turning black in color. And not only this, her eyes were turning purple, and her skin was turning green.

"Uh, Jocelyn I said, "You should check your body in the mirror." As I said this, she took out a small mirror from her pocket, and looked at herself. At first, she was shocked, but later, she smiled and said "well, I reckon the spell is over by now, foolish me, forgot to re-new the spell"

"What are you talking about" I said, "Jocelyn, I think you should go and check out a skin specialist, because, you're looking like a----like a-----"

But I was cut off by her as she said "'Looking like a witch' well it is because I am one!" as she said this, she took out a small wooden thin stick from her pocket pointed at me and lifted the stick. As she lifted the stick, I felt as if I am being lifted too, and as she shook it in a direction, I was thrown outside breaking the wall and the window, and fall down on the busy street of the town.

I somehow managed to get back on my feet. I felt a little dizzy, because I was knocked down with a very strong way of knocking down, and also that I fell 18 feet below. I quickly took lunar ray and wore it. And within fraction of seconds, it transformed back in the helmet. But it didn't gave me any information about her.

The people in the streets started panicking. They started running away shouting in a language I could not understand.

Jocelyn was a full witch by now, and she was laughing. Do you know how the female ghosts laugh in horror movies, when the female ghosts laugh with lightning strikes and all stuff and all that, well, she did the exact same, just without the lightening.

She was wearing a black long hat, and a black robe. Her skin was green in color, her eyes were purple, and her hair were short and charcoal black. When she smiled, I would see the green colored teeth, which were not neatly aligned.

"Prepare to die!" she shouted, and lifted her wand. She concentrated and her wand was covered in fire. As the wand was covered in fire, she pointed it at me, and a ball of raging fire was fired at me. But I had enough time to dodge it. She did it a couple of times too, but somehow I managed to dodge every one of them. Irritated by my constant dodging, she lifted both of her hands in the air, and started concentrated and made a fire ball at least ten foot wide. But she was taking too long. I got an opportunity to beat her.

I ran towards her, with my fists clenched, I was just a couple of feet away from punching her, when she threw the ball towards me. And the next thing I knew was that I was being burned to death.

I closed my eyes, to avoid feeling any pain, I was not in a mood of being roasted to death.

But the truth was, that I hardly felt anything, the ball just blasted away, and I was still standing as if nothing happened, and then I realized, that Marcus told me "Your Arsenal can withstand the heat of the sun till the freezing temperatures of the space."

And it was right! I didn't even feel a thing. But I celebrated way too early. Jocelyn lifted me in the air by the help of her wand, and started waving it. She was slamming me with whatever and wherever she could possibly think of. But, I was afraid that it may hit the people who were in the streets, because they were surrounding us, and some were running in any direction, and many were panicking.

And I knew, one more time if she would slam me, then I would throw up, and that too in my helmet. But luckily, before I could do so, she stopped hitting me. But it that later that I realized 'why'. The truth was that Marcus held her hand tightly, and he was Not able to move it.

"I don't think that You will be needing the wand anymore" he said, he snatched the wand and broke it in half. He was in his complete knight arsenal.

"Not my wand!!" she shouted, but it was too late.

"Now, we want some answers" said Lucius, who was right behind Marcus.

"Starting with," shouted Siegfried who was coming, "WHERE IS MY DAUGHTER!!"

The witch quickly admitted her defeat, and said, "Have mercy on me please, spare me. I shall never bring the thought of hurting you again".

"ANSWER ME!!" shouted Siegfried in a booming voice.

"Don't worry, she is in a shack outskirts of the town." She said. I could see that she was afraid, "please, forgive me."

"But, I don't understand" Said Lucius, "I thought that all the witches are extinct, then how come you are alive?"

"Who said that I am alive?" the witch exclaimed, "I am undead! I was brought back from the grave by an anonymous benefactor"

"Oh great!" I exclaimed, "So you mean that I was being attacked not by a witch but a witch who happened to be a ZOMBIE!! That's why my helmet could not tell me anything about you. Because you were already dead!"

"Well, that's one way to put it" she said rolling her eyes, "practically, I am an undead witch, because there is no such thing as Zombie-Witch"

"Lucius" said Marcus, "Find Jocelyn and bring her" and Lucius went at once. Then Marcus looked at me then he looked at the witch and said "Now, witch. Have you any idea about your prey?"

"Well, I was told, that I was supposed to kill a person who came here from earth named Nikita, apart from that, I have no Idea" she replied.

"For your information," Marcus exclaimed, "She happens to be the new Peace queen of Galdarth. In which case you have done a crime that cannot be forgiven" The witch was so scared that she was about to cry, Marcus continued "But, I won't kill you. I have made an oath, but Siegfried here never had tasted a 'sand-witch'" (this was actually pretty cool joke) "and your freedom lies in the hands of your prey Nikita. Now she will decide what to do with you.

The witch looked at me and started Crying. And I knew that she wasn't faking it. I looked her in the eyes, and I realized that I don't want to live a life full of regrets of killing, so I said, "Marcus, let her go, and give her a final warning, I am pretty sure that she won't be hunting anyone else anymore"

As I said this, the happiness of the witch knew no boundaries.

She hugged me as tightly as she could, and then blew a whistle. Right the next second, a flying broom came beside her, and she said "Broomstick, what took you so long, now don't give me the excuse that you were chatting with those mops again, were you. The mops don't love you". She said, then she thanked me, and got on the broom, she kept on continuing "I tell you broomstick, don't wipe the floors and help those mops. She doesn't love you."

She then turned to me, shouted "GOODBYE" and went away flying in the air. Marcus was looking at me the whole time. And he was smiling too. Something told me that he was smiling as if saying "good job that you spared her life. You are indeed the queen for peace"

We three went inside the Inn, as there was a commotion outside. But Siegfried managed to calm the crowd.

After this incident, the streets were almost alone, everyone was going back to their houses and those who were trying to come at the crime scene, were being sent back thanks to Siegfried. He was constantly saying to anyone who tried to see what happened or who I am. He kept on saying "Oi! Guv, go away," or "Hey you, what are you doing, don't make me throw you out." Or "Ok lads, go about your business, there's nothing to see here."

After some time, when the area was cleared, he came to our table. He was really tired, and so was I. I couldn't get a decent sleep, and now, I am constantly being watched by the pedestrians.

Lucius saved the real Jocelyn and she was in a shock. While I was very tired. She was sent back to her room to get some rest. The inn was cleared of the people, and everyone was now in their respective homes.

"Looks like the lady can do with some brandy" he said.

"No thanks, I think I can manage just fine without any alcoholic beverage" I replied.

"Marcus, a word please," Said Lucius.

"Yes my friend" replied Marcus.

They both Looked at Siegfried. He was not getting what they meant "what, you don't want me to listen". They both raised their eye brows

"Alright" said Siegfried, "I'll check on Jocelyn, you can talk in private" he went away, and as he went upstairs, Lucius said "Marcus listen, first, her majesty was attacked by demon-wolf and ogres in her dimension which breaks the laws of parallel worlds"

"Then she is constantly being attacked by bounty hunters, who aren't here just to kill her, but to kill us as well, such as the rock Giant, and those goblins"

But Marcus couldn't get it "I do not understand what you mean"

"I am saying that someone is constantly keeping out an eye for us. With each new destination, new monsters are arriving to challenge us."

"I see, now I understand the gravity of the situation" replied Marcus when he finally understood.

"And those fruits which were so disgusting, that cannot be possible, ginger woods was a holy place, its fruit should taste sweet, and moreover, it was infested by goblins. Now you know that Goblins never leave their Island, so does any other monster. They all are bound by the laws. But now, a dead witch who rose from the grave!"

"Wait a minute Lucius" warned Marcus., "Are you saying that—"

But Lucius cut it in between and said "Yes Marcus, yes. Dark powers are unleashed. There is a war coming my friend, a war far greater, for the throne of her majesty. But the question is, are we ready" (looks like I am in a jam)

Chapter 9

Things Unravel

Well, long awaited end is near pal. Good going till now, you have finally reached at a place called "And lived happily ever after" or did I said that too early..............

"So, what do you propose Marcus?" asked Lucius, "What should we do now. Our unknown enemy's turn is over, it's our turn now. What should we do?"

"First" Marcus replied, "I would like you to give me some time, the morning on the ferry will be a good time to discuss this matter, meanwhile, you both should sleep."

"Ok, tomorrow then" Lucius replied, "Good night". He said this, and went to his room. Meanwhile Marcus went towards his room, entered in it and closed the door. I slowly entered his room, and saw that he was in deep concentration.

He kept his eyes closed, and thought hard about the subject. He was sitting on a chair, in a posture that reminded me of the statue of the 'Thinking Person'

"Marcus" I said as I touched his shoulder. He was surprised to see me, because he wasn't expecting me.

"Yes, what can I do for you my lady?" he asked.

"Sorry to disturb you," I replied, "But, I don't have a place to sleep you know, can you ask Siegfried to allot me another room please."

"Yes, why not, with pleasure!" He said cheerfully and then shouted, "HEY SIEGFRIED! I need to ask you a favor my friend"

"There you go my lady" Said Siegfried as he opened the door of a common room. I entered, and thought "I really should have slept in my royal suite"

The room had one lamp, a pillow, a blanket, some haystack to sleep on, and a bucket to take a toilet break.

"Can't I just go back to sleep in my royal suite?" I asked.

"I am sorry my lady" he replied, "but the wall of the royal suite is badly damaged, and this is the best common room we have, I hope that you like it, Good night" and then he closed the door.

I rolled my eyed, and then I wanted to slam my head because of my rotten luck, but then, I couldn't be so sure about my luck, according to Marcus, tomorrow we will reach the city known as Kingslograd, and maybe, my luck changes there, so who knows, right?

I lied down on the haystack, closed my eyes, and before I knew it, I was fast asleep.

The next morning, I opened my eyes because of the constant chirruping of the birds. This time too, I didn't have a dream. But I hardly gave it a thought, I quickly got up, and washed my face, Changed my clothes, brushed my teeth, and quickly went out of the room.

Lucius was already at the table, eating his porridge for breakfast. But, I couldn't see Marcus anywhere. I sat on the table with him, and he greeted me.

"Where is Marcus?" I asked him.

"He is still in his room my lady" he told me, "Still planning what to do."

"I'll call him then" I said as I dashed upwards.

As I opened the door, I saw Marcus sitting on the table, in the exact same way as he was when I left him last night.

"Marcus," I said, "the breakfast is served, you can come down now."

"How thought full of you my lady" He said as he smiled. He came down with me, and all three of us had porridge for breakfast. While having the breakfast, Marcus talked with Lucius about what he said last night.

"Lucius" he said, "I think that you are right, but if Dark forces were indeed unleashed, should Zorodast come out of Hells-gate as well?"

"Well, I didn't gave it a serious thought," Lucius replied.

"Because if he does, than the end has definitely come, as I am powerless against his dark magic."

"I hope that you are right Marcus" he replied, "I sure do hate when I am right in these subjects"

But, then I cut them off in between and said "Whoa, whoa, time out guys, I was listening everything, what are you talking about?"

"My lady" said Marcus "before the time of unknown, there was only one ruler of Galdarth. He was a very wise and kind ruler.

His empire was so great, because at that time, this entire Planet was supposed to be his kingdom. His name was Zorodast.

But then, era of darkness was unleashed. The mighty dragon called Fafnir of the dark nation who had been sleeping underneath the very ground we all walk on, had returned from the deep slumber. He decimated jungles, destroyed villages, and killed thousands of a thousand."

"Before the knights came, Galdarth was a peaceful planet, which never had to engage in war."

"But when Fafnir was destroying the whole planet, the people had to do something. With Zorodast, and his ministers, all of them prayed for seven days and seven nights, until the Prime-angel came to them. She is a being who can fulfill any wish."

"All of the ministers asked for a race of warriors who could destroy the dragon. So the Prime-angel gave them, seventeen Elite knights, and over one hundred ranger knights, who were led by Zarthur and also told the way how to become worthy knighthood. All the knights together slew the dragon Fafnir, but, it was not finished."

"Fafnir absorbed one ranger knight from the band, and fused with him, corrupting his heart itself. He became the strongest demonic force of its time, so strong that its punches were bringing tremors to the land. He became, 'The Dragon-knight'. He decimated every knight in his path.

When the last of the knight Zarthur himself was left, then he mocked him, and punched him so hard that it proved to be fatal for him."

"The gods, who were watching together, decided to bring a new knight. All the gods from the different universe combined their powers, to make a knight whose strength will be unmatched. They gifted that power to Zarthur, making him the first of the supreme knights."

"With his newfound strength, Zarthur fought with Fafnir, and that battle is still said to be the battle of the legends. They fought for a hundred days, and a hundred nights, and till 101th day, both of them were so tired that if they would be punched another time, then both of them will die."

"So Fafnir made a treaty with Zarthur. He said that he will not destroy the planet if he gets his own kingdom. And Zarthur agreed. With his prime magicians he made a specific dimension, within a dimension, where Fafnir could rule and guard his kingdom. And being a knight of the dragon order, he gave his word."

"So, Fafnir went to the dimension known as Hells-gate, and the knights finally brought peace at last. But not for long. Zorodast wanted the power of the knights, because he knew that no one will listen as they all will follow Zarthur because of his new found power. So, he once again prayed to the Prime-angel. But this time when it appeared, it refused to give such powers in his hands, as it saw darkness in his heart. Zorodast was hell-bent, so he said that if he has darkness in his heart, then why not make him someone, who can make any other person a knight by just his will."

"The Prime-Angel was tricked, and when it gave those dark powers to Zorodast, he quickly possessed a strength that no one else could match. He became from 'Zorodast the great' to 'Zorodast the dark wizard'. He summoned some knights to his courtyard alone. And when they came. Zorodast converted them into the knights with black hearts, having the same strength, but evil mind and heart. These knights became what we call "The knights of the Dark order" or also known as "Vandals.""

"He quickly started establishing a kingdom of Vandals, and planned to infiltrate another dimension so that he could possess two dimensions for his kingdom. Fortunately, Zarthur found out about this, and was against Zorodast. This started the 'war of a hundred years' in our dimension. But luckily, the vandals were defeated by the knights, and Zorodast was sent in a prison in hells-gate. But we had no idea what to do of the Vandals, so we gave them the biggest island of our planet. Where they could live. That isle was named, 'Ragnadrake!' And we kept this huge isle called 'Knightheart' for ourselves."

"Unfortunately, this war proved too much for Zarthur. And he died, yet honorably, and his supreme helmet was passed onto his second in command. And another elite knight, became the supreme knight"

"But this was not the end of our misery, the Vandals were not so merciful, they wanted to avenge their dead, so they made their own kingdom in the west, known as 'Kingdom of Ragnadrake'. Though the knights had a treaty of peace with some of the monsters such as trolls, Demon-wolves, and Orc, yet all the Vandals cared about was to wage war against knights. So sometimes, maybe once or twice a month, they send some foot soldiers from ships which burn and pillage our villages and town. And so in return, the knights fight against them, and mostly we win"

"But if extinct monsters such as witches are re-living again, then it can only be the work of Dark powers, means that Zorodast may return again, blood-thirsty than ever." Added Lucius.

"Whoa" I replied, "That's awful lot of bad things that happen in this dimension."

"Aye" added Siegfried "AYE Aye", who was listening the conversation. But then he realized, that a man with only one eye was staring at him, so he quickly apologized. (Get it! Aye, eye?!)

"Can you help us once again Siegfried?" Marcus asked him.

"Yes, name it" he replied.

"We need to a get ticket of a ferry which crosses the Primus sea in just one day, can you do that my friend?" Marcus asked.

"Crosses the primus sea in one day!" Exclaimed Lucius, then he started thinking hard, "Well, I don't know, but I have heard about a very fast vessel called 'The flying Dutchman'".

"No way in hell!" I said as they started looking at me, "There is no way that I will board a ship infested with Pirates. I have seen 'Pirates of the Caribbean'. Davy Jones is the captain, who HAS AN OCTOPUS FOR HIS HEAD!! His crew is full of creepy Sea-Men-Creatures kind of thing. Count me off, I am not going to board this ship."

As I said this, Marcus, Lucius and Siegfried looked at each other, burst out laughing!!! Siegfried was so heavy that when he fell down laughing, the whole wooden floor creaked. Lucius just could not stop hitting the table from his bare hands, and Marcus kept on Laughing non-stop holding his stomach.

"What's the big Deal if I am afraid of Pirates?" I exclaimed, "I mean, Marcus is afraid of Goblins, why you don't make fun of him!"

After some time, when Everything was almost normal, then Marcus managed to say, "Worry not my lady, there are no Pirates in this dimension, Pirates are present only in your world, not in Galdarth, and flying Dutchman is a cruise-ship that is so fast, it feels as if we are flying."

Well, this seemed to make me laugh too. I mean, all that creepy crew, thing, wasn't here. the only person who could not stop laughing was Siegfried. He kept on falling. Then when he saw that all of us were looking at him, he quickly stopped laughing. He stood up, and straight, and said, "Apologies your Majesty, I forgot in whom presence was I" but his constant laughing had made me forgot what actually happened.

"How much time will it take, to reach to the other port?" Lucius demanded.

"Let me think," said Siegfried. He thought for a minute or two, and then added, "I think it will take at least 7 hours, but worry not, it is a cruise ship, so you will be getting your own rooms"

The next thing we all did was to pack our luggage, as we quickly came down within fifteen minutes. We all said good bye to Siegfried, and Jocelyn. And hugged each other. Marcus gave a couple of rubies to Siegfried.

At first he was reluctant to take any, but later when Marcus pressurized him, then he had to take it.

Then we went to the stable nearby and paid the stable boy with one ruby. And took Noel and Phillip with us. I hopped on my unicorn as we all made our way to the dock yard. As I looked around, I saw that the streets were much busier in morning.

Children were playing on the streets, people were selling vegetables. Some were reading while walking. And they were all greeting each other, including us.

But some were trying to avoid me. I could see that. Some were just not making an eye contact, as if they are afraid of me. I knew because of the fight with the witch. But then, most were not that rude.

One small child came near Marcus and said, "You are the supreme knight Sir Marcus! Right My lord?"

Marcus smiled and nodded, "that would be me my child" he said, "Tell me, where is your mother?"

"She is buying some vegetables from the Market!" the kid was so excited, that he could barely speak. "I have read all your battles and know almost everything about you sir. I will one day join your army my lord."

Marcus smiled gently once again "I need men like you. But for now, go and take care of your family. Be a good boy, and then join the army, ok my little friend?"

"Yes my lord" the child said. But before he could speak another word. His mother came from behind, and started scolding him.

"Arthur!" she shouted, "I told you not to wander off! Why in the name of the knights don't you ever listen to me?" then, she saw that Marcus and Lucius were standing right in front her, so she kept her mouth shut, and controlled her temper.

"I am sorry for the disturbance, my lord" she apologized, "My little son just wandered off without my knowledge, this shall not happen again Sir Marcus" she kneeled down, went took her child with her without saying anything else. She reminded me of our very cruel principle who was very rude to her own sons, she never them play video games, never let them hang out, and tells them to study 6 hours daily!!! What can be worse than that?

"But Mother!" the kid protested, "He is Sir Marcus the supreme knight! The Vandal Slayer! He fought Vandals in almost thirteen hundred Battles and never lost any one. He leads the centurion battalion! He is the strongest knight after Sir Nortus! He defeated the sea serpent with just one punch! He has defeated an army of ten thousand Orcs alone single handedly and without even being punched once. He lifted moon itself once when it was going to collide with Galdarth, and the impact could finish the life on Galdarth, he is the best knight ever! I want to be just like him when I grow up!"

But his mother gave him a menacing look which grownups usually give to their children when they speak something wrong. She whispered angrily "Wars and Knighthood are foolish things to pursue. Why do you want to put your life in danger! You will become a librarian like your father and will have a nice settled job, away from those knights and those useless wars. Now come with me young man, we need to talk on some matters such as wandering off without your mother's consent."

My mind was at two things at that moment, first was that I felt sorry for that child, and for Marcus, because he wasn't being given the respect he clearly deserved, and second, how in the name of god, Marcus lifted an entire Moon! I mean, moon is as big as the continent of Africa, at least in our dimension, but in this dimension, it is twice as big!!

We all kept on walking, while I tried to fit Marcus's strength that would somehow make logic in our universe. But, before I could reach at my conclusion (even I wasn't getting anywhere!) Lucius disturbed me, by informing me that we finally reached at the port.

The port was full of big boats, which looked like the ships from the era of the Vikings. They were at least fifty meters long and thirty meters tall, and twenty feet meters wide. The dock yard was full of people.

Some were oyster collectors, who wanted to dive in and collect oysters, others were fishermen, who were catching fishes, but they were not cutting them, or eating them, they were selling the fish as a whole, in a bowl of glass, it was later Lucius told me that these fishermen, sell fishes as pets, and sometimes as food for those who are having meat eater pets, such as having a wolf or Warg.

The port was full of people, but it wasn't crowded, we had enough space to move freely with our unicorns. There were different docks from where each vessel would leave for the port on the other side. There were big wooden Cargo ships, there were huge ships which were for the troops, and there were many passenger ships.

The Flying Dutchman was supposed to be leaving from dock 29. So, we kept on moving, till finally we found it. The vessel was majestic. Contrary to what I thought, it was more like a cruise ship. Over seventy meters long, forty meters high, and thirty meters wide. This ship was having near 50 rooms for individuals. And this ship was way better than what I thought it would be.

A young Man, who was wearing loose fitted Pajama and cloths, was at a small wooden bridge which was connecting the ground to the entrance of the ship. He had a paper and a pad with him. And he was writing the names of everyone who was buying the ticket for the ship. He was holding a black feather, but, the thing was that the man would kept on writing, and didn't bothered with ink. It was after some time, that I saw that the feather was working as a pen. It would keep on writing and writing, and it will never finish.

We came near the young man, and he greeted us with warmth. He said "hello sirs, and ma'am. How can I help you in this beautiful day?"

"Greetings friend" said Marcus, "we would like three tickets for three people, and three tickets for stables for the animals."

"Right away sir" he said. He tore of a sheet of paper, where it was written "𝕿𝖎𝖈𝖐𝖊𝖙 𝖋𝖔𝖗 𝖇𝖔𝖆𝖗𝖉𝖎𝖓𝖌 𝖙𝖍𝖊 𝕱𝖑𝖞𝖎𝖓𝖌 𝕯𝖚𝖙𝖈𝖍𝖒𝖆𝖓, 𝕹𝖚𝖒𝖇𝖊𝖗:7865". He gave no.7865, 7866,7867, to the three of us. And gave us three tickets for the stable. And Marcus gave him one ruby for that.

"But sire" the Man said, "I have not the amount of silver to give you the rest of money."

But Marcus friendly said "Keep the change,"

Marcus, took out a small silver dog whistle from his armor- jacket and blow it. And within a matter of seconds, Fang came rushing towards us. He licked Marcus with his big one foot long tongue, and pounced on him like a dog.

"Stop it Fang," Marcus said smiling. And, then we all boarded the ship. I finally stopped when I reached my room. this time, we had two adjoining rooms. I opened the door, and saw that it was just like a suite of Siegfried's inn. In addition it was having a small circular window, from where I could see the view. There were small chandeliers, which were attached to the wall. Each one was having four candles. There was a bed, beneath the bed, there was a drawer. And, there was an oil lamp beside the bed. There was my bathroom, where there was a sink, with a mirror, big enough to just see one's face in it. A bucket, which I knew I was supposed to use when I needed a little tinkle. But, a thing which made me smile was that it was having a bath tub, and hot water was available. This made me smile.

"So, I'll spend two hours in the hot tub, so great, only five hours will be left" I said to myself.

After seven hours of boring cruise, where all I could see was sea, sea, sea, and even more sea!! We finally reached to the next port.

This port was known as the 'Primus Port'. This port was just like the other one, only bigger in size. As we got down, I knew that it was afternoon, the suns were high over the head, and it was kind of hot and humid in the port. Marcus led us outside the port, where once again prairie like grasslands were present.

We got on our Animals, and went straight with all our speed. I knew that Marcus and Lucius were relieved as we were going to reach Kingslograd soon. It was our next, and Last stop. For over next couple of hours, we kept on galloping. I could see many rabbits, eagles, coyotes, even foxes. It was like the circle of nature. There were some small hills too.

Well, almost two to three hours later, I saw that we are going towards a big gate. We astonishingly were ahead of our schedule. It was not even evening at the time we reached our destination. When we were near it, then I saw a sign board bearing "𝔚𝔢𝔩𝔠𝔬𝔪𝔢 𝔱𝔬 𝔎𝔦𝔫𝔤𝔰𝔩𝔬𝔤𝔯𝔞𝔡. 𝔖𝔱𝔯𝔬𝔫𝔤𝔥𝔬𝔩𝔡 𝔬𝔣 𝔱𝔥𝔢 𝔨𝔫𝔦𝔤𝔥𝔱𝔰". Marcus smiled at Lucius. I could see that his smile was a smile of sigh.

We started waiting for the gates to open.

We made our way to the big gate. It was almost 60 feet tall, and was made of wood. And there was a 60 feet tall wall built from its edges, which were kind of Made from grey bricks. When the gates opened, then I saw two knights, who were just like Lucius and Marcus, but their helmet was of blue color. And the logo on their leather jacket was of blue color too.

They both bowed down saying the Name of Marcus, and he instructed them to get up. As we went inside. I realized that there was not just a castle, it was a big bustling city! The sixty foot tall wall encircles the entire city.

Well, the Kingslograd city was almost like the town of Draston, but the buildings here were bigger. And the people here were having a more regal behavior. Though they all were cheerful and smiling, but they moved with purpose. Whenever they looked at Marcus, on Fang, they would greet him or bow down their heads and move on as a sign of respect.

The buildings in this city were made from wood, and were painted in mostly white of yellow, and here the streets were made from red colored bricks. Almost every building was having a sign post bearing something like "𝔠𝔥𝔢𝔪𝔦𝔰𝔱", "𝔏𝔦𝔟𝔯𝔞𝔯𝔶", and "𝔒𝔭𝔢𝔯𝔞 𝔗𝔥𝔢𝔞𝔱𝔯𝔢", "𝔥𝔬𝔰𝔭𝔦𝔱𝔞𝔩" "𝔅𝔞𝔫𝔨" or "𝔍𝔫𝔫". The lamp-post were present to. It was just like Draston.

The only thing setting this town apart was the golden top of its castle, where we were supposed to go.

As we passed through the pet shop, a couple of big dogs, and other animals Bowed down. And then I realized that they must have done it for Fang. He raised his head as a sign of regal nature, and started moving in a very royal manner.

It took us at least half an hour just to reach near the castle. It was surrounded by a moat. This was in the middle of the city! The castle was huge, it was having many tall towers, and Lucius told me that the Towers were almost 200 feet high.

There was also a sign in front of us bearing "Castle Kingslograd. Home of the knights".

The castle was made from grey colored huge bricks. And just like the city, was covered with a big wall, only a little smaller with a height of fifty feet or so. In front of us, there was a big wooden gate, which was slowly leaning down. As it leaned down, its upper edge was over the banks of the ground where we were standing.

Marcus led us inside the huge castle, and the scene was Marvelous. The castle was majestic! It was so huge. There were many parts of the castle, many buildings in it.

"So your Majesty," Asked Marcus "What do you wish to see first, the palace, the castle, or the barracks"

"I never came here," I replied, "So you guys guide me"

Lucius and Marcus smiled at each other, as if they were going to show me something very cool.

But they didn't. In fact, they started with the most boring place to start with. 'The Royal Library'. But this wasn't any ordinary library. There was an entire Building dedicated to it! It was having 8 floors, and there were thousands and thousands of shelves and billions of fat books to read! There were long ladders from where one could take a book from any shelf. There were at least 100 librarians to check and make sure that there is pin drop silence. Marcus and Lucius were showing me everything they could show.

"This man" Lucius said, pointing towards an old person with a long bushy eye-brows, and wearing a strange white colored long robe, and was having a very, very long beard, it covered all of his chest and parts of is tummy. He was wearing spectacles, and as he saw me, he smiled, and came towards me. He was walking as if he was gliding in the air, as the hem of his long robe swiped across the floor.

"It is an honor my lady" he slowly said in an old man tone. He reminded me of Dumbledore from Harry Potter series.

"My queen," Said Lucius, "Meet Merlin. The Prime Keeper of the books in the royal library. He has been living in this library since the last thousand years."

"One thousand and four years Lucius" He corrected.

"So, you are like 'King Arthur' Merlin?" I asked.

"No, I am like 'Merlin' Merlin" he joked, "I know you have me confused with the Merlin of your world, but I assure you, I am nothing like him. He was a great magician, while I am a mere librarian. And a scholar." I nodded.

Then suddenly my eye went on something, that we people call a globe. This library was having a globe alright, but, I wouldn't call it the same globe as we have. Here, the globe was having a thick plate kind of thing. Not the ball shaped structure we had.

"See" I said looking at the globe, "I don't know much about geography, but the last time I saw a globe, it was consisting of a ball rather than a thick plain plate"

Merlin saw what I was saying and said "AH, your Excellency, is gifted with keen observation." He came near the globe, then said "Galdarth your majesty, is not a sphere, which has a crust, mantle, or a core. It is a huge land which is at a right distance from the suns, we have life on our planet"

I nodded, even though it was difficult for me to digest at that time. This planet was having only two continents. One was named 'Knightheart" where we were right now, and other one was called "Ragnadrake" there were also some islands, but I knew that this was the place where the respective monsters live.

Then Marcus and Lucius took me to a place they called 'Barracks,' where I met their friends who were the ranger knights. I met almost everyone who was in the 'centurion battalion'.

Barracks were actually tents where the ranger knights lived. At the time there were over 90 ranger knights, and big orange and yellow striped tents. There were near 50 tents. And on each tent, there was a flag which had the emblem, which was a knight's logo. The dragon that is pierced by two long swords.

At first, when everyone met me, they quickly bowed down. I felt kind of blushing. Because there were over 90 people who were bowing down in front of me, and the best part, FOR ME!

But, as I am not used to such behavior, it felt very awkward at that time, so I quickly ordered everyone to just stand up once again. Every one of them gave me respect that I doubted I deserve. There were also many girls. I never thought about that. The way they wore their arsenal made them look super badass. They all were just as kind as Marcus and Lucius. Though they had different behavior, they all were just as kind to me.

Then, Lucius took me to the area of the elite knights. It was basically a whole tower, with each floor for a knight. There were seven elite knights, including Lucius, who had each battalion under their command. But my arrival (as their queen) was very big issue, so they left their army at the crusader outpost, and came back to Kingslograd.

We ordered our animals to stay outside, and we three went inside the tower. Almost at every corner of the hallway, there was either a painting, or an empty armor of a knight. Lucius instructed me to stay down, and he will call the elites himself. And I did as he told me to do. Marcus went with him upstairs.

Though we were in a tower, it was not very small in width. It was one of the biggest towers in the castle, as Lucius told me. The floor was made with wood, and the walls were painted white, and after a few meters, you would see portrait of an elite knight standing regally.

But the best part was, that there was a portrait of Lucius!! And in the portrait, he made himself look way more muscular than he was. Though he had a good physique, but in the portrait he resembled a heavy-weight boxer. With massive biceps, and broad shoulders, muscular legs, and a torso full of abs.

I couldn't help myself, I tried to stop myself from Laughing, but I couldn't. And I burst out unintentionally. It made me laugh so much, that I forgot I had company. It was after some seconds that I saw that some people were in front of me. So I managed to stop my laughter.

Their faces were hidden as the sun was at their back, but as they came near, I understood who they were. They all were the elite knights. But the crazy part is, that I knew each and every one of them. The seven nights, including Lucius were those who I knew. Some of them were in my school, some were from my neighborhood.

But even crazier part was, that one of them was a girl from my class. A person I least expected (excluding that Madhav is Marcus, you know, that thing really blows my head of). The girl was none other than Jyoti!! My best friend, the craziest girl of all, she was an Elite knight!

"Jyoti!!!" I shouted as I hugged her tightly. But, when I looked at her, then I saw confusion in her eyes. And then I remembered that she is not Jyoti. Just her parallel being.

She raised her eyebrows and said awkwardly "Uh, Thank you for embracing me your majesty, but, I think you have got me for someone else."

But Lucius corrected her saying "No my love, she is not wrong. You happen to one of her best friend in her dimension."

"Wait a sec" I cut him off in between and slyly said, "Did you just called her 'my love'?" it was very unusual to see them so close together. My two best friend kissing together. The image made my stomach rumble, and I knew that if I thought about it anymore, could gag my breakfast on the carpet beneath our feet.

They both looked at each other, and then Lucius said, "Yes, your majesty, we happen to be in love with each other"

I got exited and said "So, you are like, 'love' love each other, or 'like' love each other or—"

But before I could finish my sentence, Marcus annoyingly said, "Can we carry on with the greeting please Lucius?"

"Yes Marcus" he replied, and pointed at Jyoti and said, "She my lady, is Jena. She is the first lady to ever become an elite knight, and leads the 'Eureka' battalion which consists of 32 ranger knights and is posted in the northern plains of our continent"

He then pointed at a boy who was right beside her and said "He is Dreyfus. He is second in command of the Eureka battalion" this boy is in my schools, and is one year junior to me. He happens to be schools boxing champion.

Lucius then pointed at a boy beside him and said "He is Edward. He leads the 'Prime' Battalion which has 38 knights and is posted in the western region of Knightheart." He was actually the greedy son of our wealthy neighbors, and in my dimension, he was a spoiled brat.

Then Lucius pointed at another girl, who in my world was nothing but a bunch of showoff, because she was very hot. "She is Ann your majesty. She is a new comer, and became knight just 40 years before. She is second in command of the 'Prime' Battalion"

He then Pointed at a boy beside her and said, "He is Randal. He commands the "Slayer" battalion which consist of 42 ranger knights, and is posted in the northwestern part of our continent" this guy was in my school, and was known to be a great guitarist.

Then for the last time, he pointed towards a boy (really, Lucius Points a lot) "He is William Your Majesty, he is second in command for the 'Slayer' Battalion.

They all welcomed me with warm heart. And they showed me their tower. Though there was not much to see, apart from paintings, armors, paintings, armors, etc. But I somehow stopped my erg to act as like a moron, and tried to act very knowledgeable about the paintings (this is going to be a bad idea in near future, I just know it).

Marcus then asked me if I would wish to see the King of Kingslograd, Sir Nortus. For which I said yes. But Lucius elected to stay behind saying that he needs to catch up with Jean. (You can get the idea, right)

So, I and Marcus went downstairs and started heading towards the palace. But before entering into the Palace, we were supposed leave our animals at the stable, so, we first entered into the stable.

This stable was much bigger than the stable in Draston town. It was made from bricks and mortar instead of wood and clay. Each animal had at least five to ten meter wide space, depending upon the size of the animal. There was a boundary made by bricks and the front area was closed by small steel bars together to form a steel gate, as if each animal is being given its own room.

There were horses, ponies, unicorns, but that was all animals I could find in there. This stable was also having different sections for each animal. "I think they are not supposed to bring a large variety of animals in the knight's stable" I said to myself.

First came the 'Horse section', there were hundreds of horses having their own rooms!!! Each animal had a name written over its place. Then after some time, came the pony section. Everything was same so we kept on moving till we find the 'unicorn section', then after some time we saw the name '𝔓𝔥𝔦𝔩𝔩𝔦𝔭' and '𝔑𝔬𝔢𝔩' There was some hay, bucket full of water, and an empty bucket (I don't need to tell you for what reason, right?)

There was enough hay for them to sleep on it. There was even a pillow for them to sleep!!! And an oil lamp hanging over their room each. This seemed illogical as to how can a unicorn light an OIL LAMP!!! But, in a way, their rooms were better than the 'common room' I had got at Siegfried's inn. It wasn't having a pillow.

Then, we moved on to find Fang's room. after a couple of minutes, when we passed the Unicorn section. There was a huge room where Marcus was taking Fang. In fact there were two rooms, one was well lit, other one was a big cage having a shadow over half of its area. One of them was having the name of "𝔍𝔞𝔫𝔤" and other one was having "𝔄𝔷𝔞𝔷𝔢𝔩"

As Marcus placed Fang in his room, he said "Now my lady, shall we make our way to the palace?"

But, I wanted to know what was in the cage. I was hearing some whimpering of a dog, as if he was sad. And then, I saw a figure of a dog coming out the shadow. The dog was just as big as Fang, I knew that he must be Nortus's animal. But he looked so sad, for a moment there, I almost forgot that I was afraid of dogs.

I put my hand inside the cage, but as I did Marcus shouted "No My lady, DON'T DO IT!!" and as he finished his sentence and dashed towards me, the giant dog barked and pounced at me hand. If not for Marcus, my hand would have been gone by now. At first I thanks Marcus for saving me, but then, a chill ran down my back. The dog was no ordinary giant Doberman.

It was just as big as Fang, and in addition, it had three heads!!! Each head was of the same size, and was drooling and growling at me. If one started barking, then so did the rest of them.

"My lady" Marcus said, "You should thank your stars, you were just about to be killed by a Cerberus"

"By a what!" I cried, I would hardly believe what the three headed dog would have done, if not for Marcus. Fang started growling at Azazel, which made him realize that he is not the only badass in the stable, he went back in the shadows, and started gazing me with his read eyes.

"I think that we should go to the palace right away" Marcus said.

"Good Idea" I chimed in.

We got out of the building, and made our way towards the palace. This whole castle was not smaller that a city. It was really very big, and if earth had something like this area, it would have been swarmed with tourists.

We kept on walking till we reached at a smaller yellow and golden colored Palace with large amount of cone shaped tops. Having large number of windows.

Now I find it a little difficult to tell you how the palace looked like, but, I am sure you know how they look, if you have seen any fairy-tale movie, or ever seen any animated Disney movie. If you know then picture that palace, and paint it yellow and orange cones on their top, and Voila. You have just seen the palace (and if you can't imagine, then goddamn you)

The door was at least 25 foot tall. As we stood in front of it the words read "Ra-ZE-KA-HE-SHO-PAZ" it was the same thing which Lucius said when he killed the Demon-wolf.

As we entered the doorway, and got in the palace, I realized that I was walking on cool Marble floor. The whole upper part of the palace was having large windows, and the windows had paintings, of some great battles. It was just like a huge cathedral made in gothic style.

The support pillars were present almost every 15 feet. And beside each pillar, on the ground, there were chairs. And people wearing very strange white costumes were sitting on them; they were wearing white tall cotton hats.

They all looked like Merlin of this world, in the manner they were sitting and wearing their clothes but the only difference was that they were wearing a hood. There were at least twenty chairs on each side. And their eyes were on me and Marcus.

And right in the middle, there was a high ground, where the king was sitting. He was wearing a shiny red colored crown, which was having gold colored jewels in it.

He was also wearing a long thick cape, which was of red color, and the end was of white. It looked like fur of any animal. But I wasn't sure. He was sitting just like a the sculptor of the 'The Thinking Man'

This was not surprising me, but what followed did. At first, I knew that the person sitting on the high ground throne was none other than the strongest supreme knight Sir Nortus, but I had no Idea who he might be. But now I do.

As I went near him, I saw, and gasped as chill ran through my spine, after seeing who Sir Nortus is. Sir Nortus was none other than Vishal Gulati!!!!

Chapter 10

Betrayal

See!! See!! I told you that this is very confusing yet interesting, but if you want something more, then carry on...........

At first, I was not just surprised but also confused. But, as I started to calm myself down, I soon realized that this wasn't all that illogical. Vishal was the strongest boy in our class, and there was no one who could mess with him. And Vishal would always bully Madhav. So it kind of made sense why Sir Nortus's incarnation, was actually the bully of the class.

"Nortus," Marcus said, "We have succeeded in the mission. We have escorted the Peace Queen unharmed at your palace. But I want to know, when are we going to have the royal ceremony for the crowning?"

Nortus, smiled, and started clapping. Soon every person started clapping. Nortus got down, and hugged Marcus. And Marcus hugged him back. They both started Laughing, and everybody present in the palace started cheering him. All of them started chanting the name of Marcus, which echoed through the walls.

I felt happy for him. After five days of quest, we finally reached out destination, but I did not know what they will have in store for me, and I was not sure that I even wanted to.

I was just playing along.

Marcus turned at me, held my hand and cheerfully shouted "All hail the princess!"

And everybody shouted, "ALL HAIL THE PRINCESS!!" I lost control too and laughed uncontrollably.

"Marcus my friend" Nortus said as he controlled his happiness "I am so happy for you, you almost gave me heart attack, when you didn't returned this morning, but alas, now I am at peace."

"I was afraid as well" Marcus said, "I thought the Bishops will eat your heart out if we fail." He joked. This made all the people laugh.

Then Nortus looked at me, smiled and asked "So Marcus, tell me, are you certain that she is the one?" for which Marcus told him everything about me, which matched with the girl in the prophecy. Nortus agreed, he took my hand and kissed. "I," he said, "Sir Nortus, the king of Kingslograd, is at your service" this made Marcus a little bit uncomfortable, and me too, because I was never been kissed on my hand by any one, let alone a tall handsome well built boy.

"Well" Nortus said, "I think this moment deserves a celebration. Let's have a feast tonight at the Royal Luncheon! And bring all the workers, royal family members, family relatives, Elite knights, and their family. And we all shall enjoy this night, as to the night of our salvation!!!"

This made the people in the palace even more excited! But before that, I had to be acquainted with them. Marcus told me that they are the royal bishops. They all were well over their 60s. But they had the cheerfulness of a child. They all greeted me, and told me their names.

After wards Marcus took me to 'The Tower of Royal chambers'. It was a building where there were the royal rooms for guests. As he opened the door of my room, the bag dropped from my hand. This room was huge!! As if it was made for a Giant. The room was having rooms within itself! It was having a den, with a chimney and a very comfy and beautiful sofa. There was the master bed room, where there was a big wardrobe full of beautiful dresses which I never saw in my whole life, let alone wearing them. There was a beautifully made mirror with drawers on its each side. The window was having a balcony, from where I could see that whole castle. I was given the most beautiful quarters as I could see the royal garden from my balcony. I could breathe the sweet smell of roses in the garden below. The room's interior was decorated with white and pink paint, to make it look more attractive.

But the best part was the bathroom. There was a beautiful Marble and glass made sink which was decorated with gold! The mirror was too. And the whole bath tub was made from gold!! There was also the western style toilet! This meant I could enlighten myself in peace!!!!

"So I hope that you have liked the chamber my lady" Marcus said hesitatingly.

"Like it?" I said, "I love this room!!!"

Marcus gave a sigh of relief and said "Thank god, my taste of the decoration was good"

"You mean," I asked, "You had this room made in this way just for me?"

"Yes my lady" he said as he smiled, "I did because you are a very special guest, in fact, this place was nothing, it was empty, but I had---" Before Marcus could finish his sentence, I hugged him. This made him surprised for a couple of seconds, but he deserved it. No one ever did something like this for me before, not even my parents. Marcus was a true friend, a friend I always wanted, and that's why I hugged him tightly and said "Thank you Marcus"

"For what my lady?" he asked hesitatingly.

"For everything" I said as I left him. He blushed a little, as I saw his cheek became red.

Then he said "Alright, tonight, is the Royal feast my lady, everyone expects to see the royal Princess. So, at seven o clock, three female servants will arrive to help you in dressing up. Then I will come myself at eight o clock to escort my lady for the feast.

"Got it" I said, "I will be waiting"

Marcus kneeled down, and went out from my room. He was trying to hide his emotions, but failed as I could see that he was jumping happily all the way till the stairs.

I smiled at his childishness, as I closed the door.

At seven o clock, my doorbell rang, and three palace maids greeted me. They had brought variety of corsets with them so that I could choose. Unlike the corset of our world, a 'Galdarthian corset' does not hamper your body organs, yet makes your figure seem desirable.

And I bought it in a heartbeat, not that I was very fat. I was having the most slender figure in my class, but, I was eager to try something new.

Wearing the corset was very difficult; I had to make a perfect posture for at least five minutes so that it the corset can fit on my body.

After doing such difficult task, the maids moved on. They let me choose the prettiest pink dress. It was like a big frock, having lairs and lairs of light pink color cloths beneath it. And mind you, it was difficult to wear that too. Then, when the maids were finished, they started preparing my face fit for the feast. It took almost half an hour for them, to finish my make up, but when they finished it, and I looked my face in the mirror, then I couldn't recognize myself.

I was really looking like a princess. The maids had done their jobs perfectly, no one could tell that I had done make up, but I face was definitely more beautiful than I before. My hairdo was though old style, but it was pretty, the twisted way in which my one flock of hair lied on my shoulder and the rest on my head.

I thanked the maids and they kneeled down, and left the room. At eight 'o' clock sharp, my doorbell rang again, and Marcus entered in my room. He was wearing a 16th century three piece suit, and smiled as he saw me. It was shining yellow and orange colored suit.

"How do I look?" I asked.

"Like a princess, my lady" he said, as he bowed his head down. He made me smile. He lifted his hand, as a sign of honor, and I held his arm.

We then, got down the "Royal tower of chambers" and headed for "The Royal Dining Hall". As we both walked, I saw that many other people who all were wearing 16th century party suits, in different forms or versions are heading towards the hall. Looking at all of them, wearing such strange costumes, made me feel that it was just like a fancy dress party.

All of them were gazing at us, some of the girls, who were alone, were glaring at me angrily, as if I just snatched their purse. Most of them would bow their heads a little whenever I passed them, and would say "Good evening your Majesty and Sir Marcus". I could see some girls, who bent their knees a little to show their respect, whenever they were being praised, so I started doing the same.

I saw Lucius wearing exactly the same type of dress which Marcus was wearing, just in white and blue color. He was with Jena. She was wearing a thin frock, which was shining blue, and she was wearing a beautiful necklace.

I waved my hand at them, Lucius saw me, and joined us.

"So, my lady" Lucius said, "I hope that you are enjoying your stay here?"

"Oh, yes" I replied, "I love it here, you should see my room, it's totally awesome, and it can beat any five star hotels."

He nodded.

We made our way for the dining hall. It was just like a palace, only smaller. The door way was huge, at least thirty foot tall. And as I entered, I gazed at the place. There were long dining table, and by long, I mean really very long. At least hundred people could sit on each table, and there were five of these tables!!!

Marcus chose the middle one for me. We both sat together, and Lucius and Jena joined us. This building too, just like the palace, was supported by big pillars, which were at the edge. The high ground was the dining table of Nortus. He was sitting there in the most regal and stern manner, as if boasting his power. Behind him there was his own statue built just like the one of Zarthur we saw in the town of Draston only that in this statue, he was not wearing his helmet; he held it in his one hand.

Then when all the guests were settled, he clapped his hands together, and said "Let, the feast, begin"

And as he said this, the kitchen doors open, and dozens of waiters came along which silver plates and the dishes covered in silver utensils, which are used to cover dishes. (What! I too can forget some English words ok, I am a teenager remember!)

The dishes were served, and they were looking delicious. There were mashed potatoes, spicy tofu, baguettes, croissants, boiled rice, boiled and roasted vegetables, spicy vegetables with rice, porridges, soups, salad, pancakes, pastries, cakes, pies. These guys were even having FRIGGIN' Spaghetti!!! And neither of Lucius not Marcus told me!

Then the waiters brought in hundreds of varieties of Wines. The feast started and everyone started eating from there plate. As I ate my food, I found out that it was even tastier than what Lucius could cook. Lucius was a very good cook, but this food was so delicious that I almost forgot about my rotting half-eaten sandwiches in my bag-pack.

"So tell me my lady" Ann said, who was sitting right in front of me, "You have been on earth for your whole life?"

"Yeah" I replied as I slurped a spaghetti noodle.

"So, I am just keen to know, what is the purpose for the humans of earth to use, what you people call, 'a diaper'" she asked.

I somehow managed to swallow my morsel when she asked me the question, I mean, how stupid and annoyingly curious can a person be. As she asked the question, Lucius (Who was in middle of Jena and Marcus) said, "I don't think that it is a very good topic to be discussed while having dinner."

"Why is that so?" Marcus asked him. Lucius rolled his eyes, and whispered something in his ears, and then, Marcus face turned white! He gasped, somehow, forcing himself to smile, he said, "I seem to have lost my appetite my friends, you can carry on"

I rolled my eyes and said, "That Figures".

Then Jena asked me, "My lady, forgive me for interrupting you, but, I am just curious, about how your world manages to wage so many wars, with its own people?"

I answered, "Well, I guess that our world has still a lot to learn, when peace is concerned. People bring different reasons such as religion, poverty, poor governance, etc."

"It must be difficult for you to live there, eh?" asked Randal.

"You know, not all of us like to wage wars" I replied.

"And thanks to those guys that our planet still survives" I said. But the question, just didn't stop, they kept on asking me questions like 'Have you ever been in another dimension'. And each question was weirder than the last one. They went from 'How do you spend your time In Earth' to 'Have you ever been in love.' And I answered all of their questions.

Then I said, "Alright, enough of your questions now. Now I will ask a question"

"When I first met Lucius, when he saved me from the demon wolf, he said something like, RA-ZE-KA-HE-SH0-YAZ! At first, I didn't gave it a serious thought, but then, when I was entering the palace, I saw the same Markings on the door way. What is the meaning of this phrase?"

The knights looked at each other and smiled at me. Lucius said, "You have a very good observation your majesty. But, I simply must ask Marcus to answer that question"

"Marcus was the one who created the oath" Jena added, "The oath contains what Marcus wanted every knight in Galdarth to become, a symbol of hope, peace and power."

Marcus cleared his throat and started saying.

"This my lady" is an oath that every knight should not just learn, but practice as well just like a hobby" he said, "The word RA means I am the protector of the innocent."

"The word ZE means" he said, "I am the justice of my people"

"KA means that I am the honor of my people"

"HE means I am the fury of the helpless"

"SHO means that Even though my mind is at peace"

"YAZ states that 'I shall be the nightmare of my enemies if needs be."

"This phrase all together creates the verse RA-ZE-KA-HE-SHO-YAZ. This phrase is supposed to be followed by every knight he should worship this phrase and make use of it every day for the rest of his life."

"This phrase when put together, means "I am the protector of the innocent, the warrior of my kingdom, I am the justice of my people. I am the fury of the helpless, and even though my mind is at peace, I shall be the nightmare of my enemies if needs be" he finished. He smiled awkwardly and the knights clapped.

"Here Marcus" said Lucius as he took a glass of wine "For her majesty". Everyone copied him, and they all drank the wine together. Things were going perfectly fine till Sir Nortus arrived.

"Is this seat taken my lovely?" He asked looking into my eyes.

"No, please, sit" I replied.

"Afternoon ladies and gentlemen" He said. Though sir Nortus was Vishal in our world, his voice, his behavior and even his way of talking changed.

"Afternoon sire" they all said as he sat down.

"Here Nortus" Marcus said as he gave a glass of wine to Nortus, "To your good health"

"Ah Marcus my friend," he said, "It is so kind of you." He started drinking the wine slowly. His presence was so strong that suddenly all of elite knights and the royal folks around me stopped talking.

"Nortus," Marcus said, "I think tomorrow will be the right day for her majesty to take the throne of Galdarth?"

As Marcus said this, Nortus's eyes gazed him in anger, as if there was fire in his eyes. But somehow he calmed himself, smiled and said, "You may be right my friend, tomorrow, she should take the throne. Because tomorrow is the last day for the proclamation of throne, and if it is not done by tomorrow night till 12 am, then I fear, the end is inevitable. But, I don't give it a serious thought you know"

"Uh guys," I said, "I am still on the dark side. I do not know what I am supposed to do when I will come to the throne!"

Marcus Looked at Nortus, and then told me, "My lady, when you will be proclaimed the queen of Galdarth, then you will sit on the throne where Nortus sits now, and Nortus will become a general of the Armies."

And I could tell by his that Nortus wasn't too happy because of the decision, but he still said nothing, maybe because he knew that this was the only way to save the universe.

"I think that we should wait for some time so that we can see whether the prophecy is true or not" He said.

"And get our planet destroyed?" Marcus replied, "Never". And I knew that something bad was going to happen. My spine gets tingly whenever something bad happens, and my spine is never wrong.

"You are my friend Marcus, why would you not trust me?" asked Nortus as he drank more wine, "You know, I have never believed in these prophecies, these gods, these, gimmicks, I have a plan, why not I remain the king, and try to fix the problem to the solution?"

"I am afraid that I can't take that risk my friend" Marcus replied, as he calmly ate his pie.

"Then what if, I say no, that I may not give the throne to her majesty-to be" Nortus replied.

Marcus dropped his fork, and angrily said, "You are not serious are you. Have you lost your mind? Do you know what curses will befall on the dimensions if she is not made the queen? Do not make the mistake of underestimating the power of prophecy my friend.

There was a brief silence for a moment. I was between two destructive forces that were strong enough to wipe of generations and generations of species in a single punch. And I am having my dinner in between those two forces!! Just my luck. But thank god that Nortus was only joking. After a brief moment of silence, Nortus burst into laughter and said, "I cannot believe that you fall for that old trick!!!

And soon, all the knights near me started laughing, including Marcus.

"So, tell me Marcus" Nortus said as he poured some wine in his glass, "Tell me about this new quest of yours, I want to listen to your story after all. How did you kill all those monsters such as that Rock giant, the Orc, and those Ogres?"

"That's funny, I don't remember telling you about the monsters I faced during the quest, Nortus" Marcus said in a serious tone. He was about to say more, but Nortus interrupted and continued.

"You know" Nortus said, "I always believed that we make our own fate. We are never bound by the laws of nature, or so called prophecy" as he finished his sentence, he sharply looked at me in the eyes.

Lucius whispered in Marcus's ears "Something is fishy, I told you someone was spying on us" and all of us started staring at Nortus.

"And I still believe in that thing. And I won't let anyone, and I mean ANYONE, take away my throne from me for any reasons whatsoever.

And before Marcus could say anything, Nortus shouted, "VANDALS!! ATTACK!!!" and as he said this. Over half of the people who were in the hall quickly stood up and started attacking other people. They wore brown colored specs, it transformed into a helmet. But it was of a different kind. Unlike the knight's one, this helmet was having little spikes on its top area. And there jacket was of violet color, with a black colored skull on it.

"You fool!" Marcus shouted, "Do you know what you have done, TRAITOR. You joined hands with Vandals to keep your throne! Do you know where this will lead us, to our deaths!!?"

"The only thing that I will do now is that" Nortus said, as his crown transformed into a helmet and he said "Is that I will declare you DEAD!!" he grabbed Marcus and threw him so hard that he went flying away breaking the glass top in the hall.

"Marcus!! No!!!!!!" I shouted. I was not sure that, could he even survive the attack, let alone surviving the fall. Nortus really was just as strong as I was told. But the wrong point was that it wasn't a good thing anymore.

'Is Marcus dead?' I thought to myself, 'He can't die like this, not yet, he is the supreme knight, and he cannot die'. But my thoughts couldn't do any good. Marcus was dead, Meanwhile Lucius was nowhere to be seen, and rest of the knights was captured.

And as I looked back, everything seemed to take place in slow motion. Pillars breaking, people dying, and as I looked at Nortus, I saw his fearsome eyes. His eyes scared he daylights out of me.

His helmet was different than Marcus. On the head, the crown was still attached to the helmet. As if Nortus didn't required any specs for his helmet. His crown itself could transform into his helmet.

"Vandals!!" Ordered Nortus as his helmet transformed back to his crown, "Take this infidel girl to the dungeons, and prepare for the execution, for everyone!!!"

I tried to protest but in Vain. Though the knights could hold the Vandals, but it was for a couple of minutes because without their arsenal, they were no match for the vandals who were ready to fight. And almost in no time, they defeated the Knights without even breaking a sweat.

One Vandal got near me, and as I tried to hit him, he grabbed my hand with his Iron grip. And started dragging me. He took me outside; I somehow got up, and walked on my feet. I knew that I could not fight him. Without Lunar ray, he will kill me in a jiffy. So I kept quiet and went wherever he took me.

He ordered me to get in a cellar underneath the very ground we are walking. He somehow found the doorway, it was very dark, and all I could see were stairs. So he held my hand even more tightly. I knew that if he tightens his grip, my bone with break like a toothpick.

As we got down, I could see some light. There were flame torches attached to the walls, so that we could see. I saw that there were lots and lots of cells, but there was hardly any person in them. Yes, there was no one in the cells, but instead of people, some cells were having skeletons!!!! This made me shrill and the Vandal said, "Don't shout, you shall be joining them tomorrow, so try to get friendly with the ghosts, and skeletons."

"Wait a minute, you said skeletons and Ghost" I cried, "You mean there are ghosts down here!"

"I have been told that this area is haunted by the ghost of the Knight of the screaming world." Then he opened one cell, where there was no skeleton, just a hard floor, "I hope that you enjoy your stay," he laughed menacingly as he went away. There was nothing in the cells; the only light that could come was from the flame torches that were outside my cell.

I went near the bars so that I could be as near to the light as I could. Because I had no intention of talking to a ghost Knight. The flame flickered as tears were rolling down from my eyes. Marcus sacrificed so much just so in the end he could be killed by his own friend. The thought made me cry, because I had a feeling that this was the end.

Then suddenly I heard the gate of the dungeons, and footsteps of some people. They closed in as I backed away from the bars. And as the person stood in front of me, I realized that it was Nortus with two vandals on his each side.

He looked and me, and shook his head, as if pitying on me.

"You really thought that you could become the queen!!" He asked in a very sarcastic manner.

"Why!" I asked, "Why did you do this? I never wanted to come to throne, then why did you have to do this?"

"You think I will let you have my throne so easily!" he said, "You think that I will hand you the powers of our world so easily?"

"You sound as if there is a choice?" I snapped.

"Yes there is" he said calmly, "As earth is a master planet, I shall destroy it before the supernova can. When this happens, there will not be any logical reason for the destruction of earth. And being a master planet, and then being destroyed by the warriors of parallel universe, there will be nothing for supernova left, to be destroyed, and Galdarth will remain safe."

"So you will wipe out the face of life from earth just so that you could keep your throne!!" I shouted.

"Call it what you like" He replied, "The destruction of earth is a trifle sacrifice, when compared to hundreds of parallel universe's safety. All I need is to wait for the army of Vandals to get ready, which will happen in tow-three days, and then, we shall open the portal to your world, and destroy the life on earth. But this isn't all, I will let my Vandals have all the fun, and when they are finished, all it will take is my one mighty punch, and your earth will be destroyed in seconds." And he turned and started to leave.

"I despise you!!!" I shouted (So what if I used the word 'Despise'?), "But then, this doesn't surprise me it's coming from a person who could kill his own friend for personal gain."

This Made Nortus mad. Within fraction of second his crown transformed into his helmet and he shouted "HOW DARE YOU!!!!" his shout was so strong that it made the wall of the dungeon shake, "You think that I am his friend, Marcus was a fool to think so. He killed my brother!!! He killed my Father! I have now taken the revenge of their deaths as Marcus is now dead. They may sleep in peace now."

"I would hardly call that a fight, you killed Marcus off guard, even a ranger knight could have done that!" I declared.

He looked at me angrily and said, "Complain all you want, but by tomorrow, you will be standing in the middle of the castle, with an army of Vandals looking at you, as Azazel the Cerberus tears your soft flesh, and eats your heart. I would like to see that." He then turned back and said, "Enjoy your stay here, while you still can" and sarcastically added, "My lady!" and the Vandals started Laughing on his comment. He ordered a third Vandal to stay and Guard my cell.

I wanted to snap his neck, but I knew I couldn't even if I was out, I knew that. But I had to devise a plan, before the dawn, or this time I was sure that there was no one to save me. But before, I could think something else. The Guard Vandal fell down on the ground; someone grabbed his neck, and snapped it.

At first I was afraid that it was the Ghost Knight coming down to haunt me, but who actually came made all my tears go away.

It was Lucius!!

He saved me once again. He was wearing his complete Arsenal. His white colored helmet, black biker jacket, black pants, and black old man shoes. He grabbed the bars, and stretched them and if breaking a straw. It gave me enough space to get out of the cell. And as I got out, I hugged him as tightly as I could.

"Thank you so much" I said.

"I am just doing my duty, your highness" He replied.

He then showed me that he brought my arsenal, he even brought my bag from my room!! I was having Lunar ray once again.

"I think that we should hurry" stated Lucius, "Noel and Phillip must be waiting"

"You have brought Noel!!" I said excitedly. He hurried on our way back to the stairs. I was skipping a stair of my each step, even though I was wearing heals. But, in a couple of minutes, we reached at the top. Opened the door of the dungeon, and got out.

Lucius was acting just like a spy in a movie. He was aware of every step he made, and as we got out of the dungeon, we went near a dark place besides a building. Phillip and Noel were hiding there. We got on our unicorns, and dashed on our way towards the castle bridge.

"The bridge is still down your majesty" Lucius said, "But, as per the rule, it closes in about next one minute, so I advise you to hurry". We both increased our pace, but we were late.

The bridge was being lifted up automatically. We were late, but Lucius being an optimistic, said, "We can still make it." So both of our unicorns increased the pace, the gate was almost half way on the top.

But we still stepped on it, as the bridge was ascending, we were running on it, and as we reached at the very edge of the bridge, our unicorns jumped as high as they could. The bridge was behind us, the moat was beneath us, and we were at least 30 feet of the ground, and a thought came to my mind, 'Lucius, if we don't survive this fall, then I will kill you"

But, somehow, even though I was shouting my head off Phillip and Noel still Managed to Land on their feet, and we made a dash for it. The city was very ghostly by now. There was no one on the streets. The shops were closed; libraries were closed, as if everyone in the city knew that the Vandals have attacked the castle.

Luckily, the gate of Kingslograd was still open, so we made a dash right outside the city gates, in to the big open prairie grounds. We rode for almost quarter of an hour, till we reached at a fireplace, near a hill. It was presumably a safe place as the hill was covered with trees so no one could see us.

As I got down, I saw that there was a mushroom soup was being cooked, and Fang was sitting down. And I hate to say this but it was the first time ever when I was delighted to see the big wolf.

He ran towards me, and licked, and I too hugged him like a puppy, but the thing I was most happy was when I saw that...

Marcus was Alive! He was wearing the complete knight Arsenal.

His red colored helmet, black biker jacket, black pants, and black old man shoes

As I saw him, I ran towards him and embraced him. He hugged me back, and then I asked, "How did you survive the attack by Nortus?"

"I was wearing my jacket armor underneath my suit, so, I could survive the attack from Nortus."

When everything was settled, and I changed my clothes, (without showing anyone, and all alone this time), Lucius asked Marcus, "So, Marcus, I have brought Your Majesty as you said. Now what will we do."

Marcus replied, "Lucius my friend, tomorrow at dawn, we shall go to war!"

Chapter 11

Clash of the Legends

"No Marcus, you can't." Lucius protested, "You may manage to defeat the vandals all on your own, but I know, that then you will get so exhausted that Nortus will kill you!"

I sat near the fire place listening to their argument.

"But then what other alternative do we have Lucius?" Marcus asked, "I am the only one in this world who can challenge Nortus in strength. And even if I die, then you will have enough time to proclaim the throne to her majesty, and then everything will be set in order. Even if Nortus proves to be stronger than me, I can hold him for at least that much time."

"But that will be a suicide Marcus!" Lucius added, "You cannot fight him like this. He will kill you, and even if her majesty takes the throne, then there is no guarantee that Nortus will listen to her, if he can go against the prophecy, then he can go against her as well"

"My sacrifice will not go in vain my friend," Marcus replied, "When her majesty will become the queen, then you can call all the knights from the continent, so that they can attack Nortus together."

"And lose the defenses of our shores; we are playing too much at stake." Lucius corrected him.

Marcus closed his eyes, so that he can think of a new plan, but he was out of plans now, "Goddamn it!" He cursed, "Nortus, my brother in arms betrayed me, after what I have done for him, and he does not know how to stop the apocalypse. He will die, and take all of us with him. He planned it from the very first day he came to throne. He sent me off for wars so that one vandal, Orc, or a giant manages to kill me, but I was far better than his expectation. But I could have never thought about the end this way. That's why he gave me this quest, that's why he sent the monsters, demon wolf, ogres, Orcs, rock giants, goblins and that witch so that any one manages to kill me. With me gone, no one could oppose him. If only I'd be wiser to know about his plan, we never had to see this day. Now half of my battalion is dead, and half is in the dungeons, and that is all because of me! Maybe I should have killed him on the day I killed his brother. But now, if I fight him, and he kills me, then at least I will have paid for my mistake."

Marcus's words were echoing in my mind, that he was a good-for-nothing-failure. I got near him and said, "Hey, you think you had a hard time because your friend betrayed you, back on earth, this happens almost every week to me!"

Both Marcus and Lucius looked at me in amazement, and said, "How strong your heart is my lady, to take on such betrayal, can you please tell us the reason for such strong heart"

"I have two words for you, Marcus" I said, "MOVE-ON, it was you who destroyed the entire army of Orcs alone, it was you who saved me a couple of times, it was you, who defeated the rock giant alone without breaking a sweat. And still you think you have no chance against them?"

"You don't understand my lady," Lucius complained, "Though Marcus is strong enough to take on an army of Vandals, he is not strong enough to take on Nortus as well at the same time, and he will die in the fight. We have no army, we have no air support from the phoenix or any other animal warrior who can give us an advantage from the sky, and we don't even have a messenger. Because if I enter the city, then Nortus will kill me, and if Marcus enters the city then the fight will prolong for so long that the whole city will be destroyed. We are completely out of plans"

"So you think that you don't have an army?" someone said in a very booming tone. But I knew that I had heard that voice someplace else before, I knew that, but where.

Then before I could think anything else, the trees nearby started rustling, and then I heard the sound 'thud' as if someone was moving.

As I got up, I smiled, because I knew who it was. It was the same ENT whom I met in the Beetle woods. The one who told me about the prophecy. But this time, he could walk, his roots were twisted together to make his own two legs, and his branches were joined together to make his arms, hands and fingers! Back in the woods, he was not taller than 30 feet, but now with legs, he was over 50 feet!

"ENT" I called, "What are you doing here?!"

"We Ents hate to go to war," he said in his same old booming voice which was very slow, "We are of peaceful nature, but if the subject is concerned with our peace queen, then we can go if we must"

"Wait a minute" I said, "Did you just said we?"

"Yes" He replied, "I have brought my friends with me." And as he finished his sentence, I heard more 'Thump' 'Thump' sounds, and within a, matter of minutes the whole area was covered with dozen of dozens of ENT. Of different varieties! Chestnut, Mahogany, Ash.

"Well, now I think we have an army, don't you think so Lucius?" I said happily.

But he was still not satisfied, and he said, "But we still lack the air support Your Highness, we do not have any air support, and we do not have more than 50 ENTS here."

Suddenly, just as when Lucius finished his sentence, I heard A strong whistle, and a menacing laughter after that, and the voice said, "Did I hear someone saying Air support?" and as I looked upwards, I smiled again.

It was the same witch whom I left alive in the town of Draston. But she was not alone, after a second or two, even more witches started following her! Over eighty witches followed her as she got down from her broom, and came to us.

She bowed down, and so did all the witches, and she said, "My queen, you spared my life back there, even though I was ordered to kill you, and for that, I and the witches of Galdarth, pledge an Allegiance to you, that you give us the honor of serving your army in the battle my lady"

I raised her up, and said, "You came back, but I won't be leading the Army, Marcus will." And I pointed towards him.

"So what do you say Marcus," said Lucius, "We have got a pretty decent army now, what is your thought about it."

Marcus thought for a second and then said, "I hope not to break your hopes my fellow Ent's and witches, but it will be better if you don't go to this war, as this will bring nothing but pain and misery in your life, and I can't afford that."

"My Sire" said the ENT, "We are not asking you to lead us, we are telling you, because morality is a medicine best given to those who wish the same. Nortus is someone, who wishes to exploit your morality for his benefits, which will lead us to our doom, so please, let us fight with you."

Marcus again thought about it for some time and smiled at the ENT, and then he said "my dear ENT, you speak words of wisdom, and thanks to you I have got a new and a better plan. And you helped me in doing that"

"I-I did?" the ENT asked pretty confused.

"Yes my friend, just wait till you hear it, but for now," he said, and called a witch and ordered her, "you become my messenger, and tell lord Nortus that I am still alive and well, and that I challenge him to a duel."

Lucius tried to stop him but Marcus won't budge, as he continued, "Tell him that if he fights and wins, then he can do whatever he wants to do with me, and he can remain the king, but if he loses, then the throne will be proclaimed to the rightful successor Nikita, our peace queen, and he will be given exile. Can you do that for me?"

The witch kneeled down, whistled as her broom got near her. And after getting on the broom, she rode towards Kingslograd.

And after about half an hour later, she came back.

"Thank god sister" said another witch, "we were afraid that Nortus will capture you"

"No, Nortus is at ease" she said, "But he now knows that her majesty is not in the dungeon. He also said that he will fight Marcus. But there will be a slight change of plans, he said that if he wins, then Marcus will have to kill her majesty with his own hands" and as she said this, every one let out a gasp, then she continued, "Then, he has to watch as his friends will be executed in front of him, and then, he will have Nortus's permission to die."

Marcus thought about it for a while, and then looked at me in the eyes, and winked. Then he said, "Done"

But Lucius was angry now, "I told you, you cannot over power his army while fighting Nortus. And you know that he never fights fair"

Marcus calmed Lucius down and he said, "Worry not my friend, who said that I will let him fight by using unfair means this time?" as Marcus said this, Lucius calmed down. Then he said to everyone, "All of the warriors of her Majesty's service, we shall sleep peacefully tonight, as tomorrow, victory will be ours!!!

And everyone cheered as Marcus stopped saying. Then after an hour, everyone, including the unicorns, witches, ENT, all got ready to sleep.

Marcus tried to devise a plan to attack for tomorrow. I went near him and asked, "Won't you sleep tonight Marcus?"

"I shall my lady" He said, "But for now, I am sharing my plan with Lucius" he smiled at me as I lied on my bed. I was sleeping near the fireplace, so the light was not letting m sleep. I got away and closed my eyes, and before I knew it, I was sleeping. But this time I once again had a dream/vision in my sleep.

I saw that the whole area was covered in dead bodies. Bodies of knights, bodies of my friends, of my parents, of my teachers, of the ENT, witches, animals, vandals and what not, were lying down.

Then suddenly the whole sky turns blood red, and there is no place to run. A huge meteor is falling right at me, and lightning strikes are against the meteor, trying holding it, but it is too late, and as the meteor touches the ground, the entire planet Galdarth gets destroyed.

"My lady" I hear a familiar voice calling me, "My lady" I heard it once again. Then as I open my eyes, I see Lucius is trying to wake me up. "Get up," he said, "Nortus has accepted the challenge!!"

I quickly got on my feet, brushed my teeth, and got ready to see the fight. I saw from the hill top that Marcus was standing right in front of Nortus, and they were talking about something. This seemed reasonable, but what didn't seemed reasonable, was that Nortus had brought his entire Army to help him!!!

I put on lunar ray, and did a head count, and it told me:

NUMBER OF VANDALS: 140

BARBARIAN: 100

ELITE: 40

"Hey," I snapped, "Where are the witches and the Ent?"

"Marcus's plan do not require them my lady" he replied, as we got on our respected unicorns"

"His plans... wait WHAT!!!" I exclaimed. I mean, after so much thinking, this was his Master plan, to fight someone who is just as strong as him plus an entire army!!! I think after last night, he must have got a loose screw.

But then, I didn't say anything, because Marcus always has something up his sleeves. We made our way down the hill, right in front of the army of Nortus.

Marcus and Nortus both were in front of each other; even thought the distance between them was at least 15 meters.

As we got to Marcus, he smiled at me, and said, "I hope I will be having your blessing today your Majesty"

I nodded for an answer. Just as when Nortus saw me, he gave a menacing villain like smile and said, "You know Marcus, may be, I won't let you kill her after all. I will use her as my slave" and he bit his lower lip as he said that.

Lucius was losing it. He was getting angry at Nortus as he whispered, "Just wait you traitor, you will get a fitting end for folks like you."

Then Marcus looked at us and said, "I think that you both should go a lot farther from this place. At least quarter of a zilo far from this place will be good." He turned at Fang, and hugged him, and said, "I will always love you my faithful friend, no matter what happens." He turned to Lucius, he shake his hand and said, "It has been an honor serving at your side my friend", for which he replied, "It has been an honor to be in yours" he then looked at me, and saw a little tear rolling down from my cheeks. He wiped it, and hugged me. Then he told us to go away.

It took us a little less than five minutes to reach at the specified distance. I took out lunar ray, and wore it. It zoomed the battle field and I could even hear their voices. Just as Nortus's crown transformed into his helmet, so did Marcus's specs

"So Marcus, tell me?" asked Nortus, "Are you ready to die?"

"Funny it seems to me" Marcus replied, "You know the rock giant asked me the same thing, and later I beat him by hardly breaking a sweat."

Nortus got angry and exclaimed, "Must I always prove my superiority to you Marcus?"

"Why," Marcus snapped, "Are you afraid to?"

Nortus could take no more and said, "Shall we"

"Lets", Marcus replied, and they both sprinted at each other. And as they slammed their foot on the ground, a strong energy force emitted through the air followed by a shockwave as they punched each other.

They both were so strong that the fight was going to destroy Galdarth any way, only if it continued for days. Nortus kept on attacking Marcus, but Marcus was able to block or dodge it. But with each punch of Nortus, which was wasted, ended up emitting an energy wave. But soon Marcus was pinned again the huge hill at his Back, and Nortus at front. Just as Nortus tried to kick Marcus, he dodged it, and the kick of Nortus destroyed the hill, in just a matter of seconds!!! Where there was a big hill just a second ago, now, was nothing but debris and rubble.

Nortus got the opportunity he needed. He grabbed Marcus from his shoulders, and threw to the hill nearby. Just as Marcus's body was slammed against the hill, the whole hill broke down into big boulders of lands.

Marcus somehow got up, he was greeted by a strong kick of Nortus, but Marcus managed to dodge it.

They both kept on fighting, but Nortus seemed to have had the upper hand. His punches were making a difference on Marcus. Because he could no longer block them. I knew that his hands were aching, but he had no choice. Then all of a sudden, Nortus grabbed Marcus from his head, and slammed it on the ground. It was so strong that it made a mini crater on the ground!!!

"You know that I am much stronger than you Marcus?" Nortus said, "For how long can you play this game with me?"

"Game!!" Marcus exclaimed, "GAME!!, you thing this is a game, if so, then you ought to know that I am just beginning to play it" and just as he finished his sentence, he ran so fast that I could hardly see him, and he punched Nortus out of nowhere right on his face. And a strong shock wave emitted from his punch.

Nortus flew due to the impact force and slammed against another hill. And once again, the hill broke down. Then, Marcus landed a strong blow right on his abdomen, and I knew that Nortus has bitten more than he could chew. But I again underestimated him.

Nortus once again started fighting head to head with Marcus, and then I saw from ultra vision of my helmet, that Nortus was smiling while fighting Marcus, but then when I looked at Marcus, then I saw that he was smiling too! They both were fighting to end each other's life. They were giving everything they had on each other, punches, kick, slams, locks, everything, but none of them was going to back down.

Both of them kept on fighting, and got hold of each other's hand, as if they were wrestling. Their power was shaking the entire land, they were so powerful. Then suddenly Marcus said as he held Nortus's hands, "You know one thing Nortus," Marcus lifted him and slammed him. He put his foot against Nortus's chest, not letting him get up and said, "I should thank you for sending me to fight the battles with the vandals, at least I could remember my training as a knight, while you did nothing apart from enjoying for the last 168 years on your throne, and you have forgotten everything. That's why the chances of your winning are not as high as they should be."

But Nortus looked calm as he said, "Why do you think I brought an entire army of Vandals with me," and then he shouted, "VANDALS ATTACK!!!" as he said this, the vandals started running at Marcus to kill him.

But Marcus really had planned it all neatly, and as the Vandals approached, he shouted, "ENTS NOW!!!!!" and as he said this the Ents came out from the rubble of the hill which were destroyed and started attacking the Vandals, they would hit them with their branches, they would step on them, and they also grabbed them with their roots and threw them away.

But soon, the huge force of vandals were proving to be strong for just 50-60 Ents. But Marcus had another plan. He knew that the Ents won't be able to do much good, so he shouted "WITCHES, KNIGHTS! ADVANCE!!!" and as he said this, the knight from Kingslograd, and the witches attacked the vandals from behind. And now that's what I call a 'Master plan'

"You!!" Nortus shouted, "YOU TRICKED ME!!"

"Well," Marcus calmly said, "A subject in which you are an expert I presume?"

But Nortus without giving a warning started pounding Marcus. He didn't even gave Marcus a chance to defend himself, and kept on punching and kicking him. With each punch which landed on Marcus's body, a huge shockwave emit. And I knew Marcus couldn't take much more of that.

Their fight was so intense that the war between the vandals, and knights, Ents, and witches was over, as all of them started looking at the fight.

"I will kill her Marcus" Nortus shouted as he Punched him, "I will tear her heart out and feed it to Azazel!! And there is nothing you can do about it."

And just then, Marcus grabbed Nortus's punch and he said, "Don't you dare touch her." And slammed him. But Nortus returned the favor by punching him again and said "You are nothing Marcus, you are nothing but a warrior trying to prove himself worthy to be a king"

And then Marcus said, "I'd prefer remaining a knight" and started pounding Nortus.

This time, Nortus could hardly do anything. Marcus went berserk, slamming Nortus again and again.

Punching him non-stop, and then just as when Nortus could take no more, Marcus grabbed him and said "Time to return the favor for last night Nortus" he grabbed him, and threw Nortus so high that no one could see him.

The next minute, I sat on Noel, and went towards Marcus, with Lucius.

Everyone was so happy, as we thought we won but then, suddenly the sky became blood red, just as I saw in my dream.

And then I heard laughter of Nortus, which filled the sky, and then it said, "Marcus, you are a fool, do you know why I never used my supreme attack, because my attack was 'Meteor punch!' and I never attained the height to use it, but thanks to you, now I shall kill all of you. I WILL KILL ALL OF YOU TODAY!!

And then I saw that Nortus was fully covered in fire, and was approaching right at us. Everyone started panicking. People in Kingslograd were crying, because according to Nortus, he could destroy the whole planet!!

But Marcus calmed down, and started thinking. Nortus was closing near. And then Marcus got it. There were lots and lots of lightning in the sky, as the clouds were moving away from the area.

Marcus ordered us to back away, and he contracted all the power in his fist. He kept on contracting till hi fist was covered in lightning strikes. I was so amazed that I wanted to touch it, but Lucius stopped me as he said that the lightings in Marcus's hand was ten times more dangerous than real lighting.

As Nortus approached near, falling from the sky, Marcus concentrated even more. And then, I saw, that the lightning strikes in the clouds were getting attracted towards Marcus. And suddenly, Marcus's whole body was shot down with multiple lightning strikes, until his body was covered in lightning itself. His whole body was covered with more and more lightning. It was increasing. His eyes became electric blue, his body itself emitted lighting strikes. His eyes were now white in color dangerously white, and as Nortus approached near, Marcus Jumped as high as he could, and they both punched each other.

As they punched each other, for at least half a minute, everything was turned blank. Then when I opened my eyes then there was neither Marcus, nor Nortus.

I thought that he was dead, and I was so sad that I was about to cry, but then Lucius pointed up, as everyone including me looked upwards. And then I saw Marcus falling down with Nortus. Marcus helmet was still on his face, but Nortus's wasn't.

His helmet was transformed into his crown, and was falling down with him.

Before I could think of anything else, Marcus landed right in front on the army, but Nortus wasn't so Lucky. He landed on his back. But, his right hand was not in a good shape, apart from his whole body being ok, his hand was transformed into a statue because of extreme pressure, and overloaded power.

"Finish me!!" Nortus declared, "Finish me like you Finished my brother." His whole face was swollen, and his one eye was black and blue.

"I would" Marcus replied, "But I cannot, I took an oath that I shall never kill again, and I hope that you will learn a lesson from this." He stepped on Nortus's hand, and crushed it as if crushing an ant. And Nortus screamed in pain.

Then Marcus Took his crown and broke it as if breaking a ceramic plate and said. "And I hereby declare you unworthy of the king's title, and you shall spend the rest of your days in exile. Your punishment, is not death, but your own life."

Marcus tried to help Nortus in getting up, but Nortus refused and snapped, "I will return one day Marcus, my thirst for revenge is not quenched, I shall avenge my brother, and kill you and your friends and your princess"

Marcus calmly replied, "And I shall always be there to protect them my old friend".

Nortus shouted "AZAZEL!!" and just in another ten seconds, his faithful three headed dog appeared. He got on his dog by the help of his one arm alone, and looked at Marcus and me with cold eyes, and went away riding in the horizon.

Marcus turned back to his warriors, Smiled, and shouted "Victory!!!!" and everyone cheered.

Chapter 12

Home at last

A happy ending at last, and this is the truth! Well, I just don't want to make you angry, so why not carry on.....

Well, the rest of the day didn't do that bad, I mean, we defeated Nortus, and exiled him, we defeated an entire army of Vandals, and just after a couple of hours later, Marcus threw a party as celebration!!! These guys are really party animals, I mean they have a party almost every week, and they are still not bored from it.

After the party, when the evening came close, I went to my room so that I could change my clothes for the proclamation of the throne. After half an hour later, Marcus took me to the throne, where I sat comfortably, like a princess, and called the prime scholar Merlin.

The old man walked, holding a scepter horizontally in his hands. He bowed down, and gave the scepter to Marcus. Marcus bowed his head down as a sign of respect. And then held the scepter. He took it, and brought it to me, as he kneeled down near my legs he said, "By the power of the holy scepter, by the shine of the two suns, by the beauty of the sacred moon, by the help of the benevolent gods, I proclaim, Nikita Mehra as the Peace queen of Galdarth!"

He gave me the scepter and as I held it, I felt a new surge of power within me. As if this power would consume me. But it didn't and after a couple of seconds later. The whole palace that was crowded with people, started cheering and chanting my name. But this was not it.

Marcus took me to the palace's tower, and as I leaned on the window, I saw that there were millions of people, Ents, witches, knights and god knows who were chanting my name. And it was the first time in my life that I felt very important as a part of a civilization.

On the same night, I restored the balance of nature. And to be true, even I don't know how, the knights took me to the sick ginger woods, infested with goblins, and all I just softly touched the ground from the end of my scepter. The goblins flew away from the ginger woods, and the fruits were tasty again. And for the next couple of days, all I had to do was to sit or ride Noel.

But after some days it was very boring. And besides, Marcus had no time for me, so there was no reason for me to stay, so one morning, I called the bishops, the elite knight (Including Lucius) and Marcus the supreme knight.

"Hey everybody" I said softly. The moment was so awkward that all they did was to look at my face. A sound of a cricket and it would have been a perfect scene of a comedy film.

"I called this meeting" I continued, "to tell you that, I want to go back to earth". And as I said this, the people in the palace started creating hullaballoo. No one was listening to me, and all I could say to them was "Hey-", but they were still talking, "Now wait-" they still didn't stop, "Listen to me please-" but they kept on talking on this matter with each other, and so I lost my temper and shouted, "NOW WILL YOU ALL SHUT THE HELL UP!!!"

And surprisingly, there was pin drop silence in the palace, (Now I know how teachers feel like, and why they keep on shouting all the time) "So, what I am saying is," I said, "I need a few months off you know, I haven't seen my parents in like ten days, they must be worried sick you know, I just want to go back and tell them that I am fine"

"There won't be a need to" Merlin said.

He showed a small flask having green colored liquid, the same which brought me here. "This, My lady, will not only transport you back to your dimension, but also at any time you want. This is not like the other one, I have modified it myself"

"So you mean, I can go back to any day I have lived till now? And my parents will never know that I was in other dimension?" I asked, for which he nodded.

"That's a great way to go back" I murmured, "But, I still cannot live here forever, I have to go back, I have my own life there back on earth, and no matter how bad it may be, I have my family, my friends there, so, I can't just live here, but worry not, I have a plan for you guys"

The bishops and knights looked at each other, as I said, "This little plan is called 'Democracy'! Now all you have to do is choose the most worthy candidate among yourselves, so that you may 'Temporarily' rule Galdarth. But mind it, I'll be back in a couple of months to check on you all ok. Now those, who are in favor of this, raise your hands" and to my astonishment all of them agreed, but they also said that they cannot choose their ruler, so I have to choose it for them. And all the bishops stood right in front of me. It was difficult to choose among them because I hardly knew them.

And then it hit me, 'Why not I choose someone whom I know?' I thought, and I said, "I choose Marcus, the supreme knight, and Lucius the elite knight to temporarily become the rulers of Galdarth."

As I said that, all the bishops, almost dropped their jaws, and the happiness in Marcus and Lucius's eyes were un-describable. I did what they both truly deserved. So the next day, the scepter was locked in my own private chamber, as I left the room and all the DRESSES in it, but then I realized that if I am the princess, and if those dresses are mine, then no one will complain if I take my own dresses with me, and I did exactly the same.

Marcus and Lucius were proclaimed the kings next day, and a bug party was held, Again. In this Party, there was a ball dance too, so I and Marcus danced till my feet started to ache. And we had a great time together. After that day, I packed my bag, and stuffed it with some of the most beautiful dresses I could find.

As I was going, I could see lots and lots of sad faces, which made even me sad. I went to the highest tower to say good bye to the people for one last time, and they all shouted 'GOODBYE' to me together.

My backpack was ready, and the palace was full knights, and bishops. Lucius just could not stop the tears rolling down from his cheeks, and even Jena could not console him.

I dropped the green colored water on the floor, as it transformed into shiny green colored mirror, I saw everyone's faces for a last time before going. And I saw that Marcus was trying to control his grief. I went to him, and embraced him as nicely as I could, and he did that too.

"You know" I said, "Long distance relationship isn't very bad"

"I can see why my lady" he replied. I kissed him on his cheek, and went towards Lucius. I hugged him as he wiped his nose with a napkin.

"Here take this" he said as he gave me a normal mirror and a small flask of green color liquid in it.

"What does it do?" I asked,

Marcus replied to that one saying, "You can contact us whenever you want to, all you have to say is 'Mirror mirror in my hand, show me someone far from the land' and whoever you wish to talk to, will be able to see you through this mirror, just like you see will see them. And the flask is to whenever you wish to come back, you can drop it on the floor, wait for it to transform into a mirror and then jump into it. And the next thing you know is that you are at your throne.

"OH thank you so much" I thanked him, and hugged both of them. I placed the mirror and the flask in my bag.

Then I went towards the green mirror, looked at both of them as they said, "Farewell" together to me, and I jumped in the mirror, as everything went black.

The next thing I knew was that as I opened my eyes, I was back in my room, wearing my school uniform. At first I was confused as to whatever happened with me was a dream or not. I quickly opened my window, and saw that the sun was in perfect condition, normal yellow star as it should be.

I let out a long sigh, as I thought that all of this was a dream, but then what I saw next, almost made me jump in happiness, I saw that nearby a tree in front of my house, the headless horseman was standing, as if guarding me. No one could see him. Many passed him but no one even bothered to even see him. Because he was invisible to earthlings. Only those who could jump from dimensions could see him.

He kneeled down as a sign of respect, and I did the same. Then I closed the window, and checked my bag. There were no books in it, but my dresses of fairy tale!!! There was green colored water in a small flask, and my mirror. But the worst thing was my five days old waste sand-witch about which I forgot to eat.

YUCK!!

Then as I was changing my clothes, the surface of the mirror started rippling like water, when I smoothly touched it with my fingers, then it rippled again like water, but as it calmed down, I saw Marcus and Lucius and couple of more knights trying to see me from Galdarth!!!

"Greetings, My lady!" Marcus said as he smiled, "How are you?"

"I feel great!!" I said cheerfully,

"My lady" Nortus added, "We seemed to have a problem, you see, some of your dresses have vanished. Do you know where they are?"

I hesitated for a while but then I told them the truth. And once again, they both started laughing. I was so happy that I joined them too!

Then Marcus said, "My lady, as I see it, those dresses were yours anyway"

I nodded.

"Now when should we call you?" he asked, "There seems to be the problem in Rigyard village, looks like some trolls have attacked there. I will send a small troop of knights there. But it will take me some time. So after what time should I call you?"

"After a couple of hours" I advised, "I need a lot of catching up with my parents."

"Yes I can understand" Marcus replied, but then Lucius said, "If I am not interrupting Marcus, CAN WE GO NOW!!"

Marcus nodded and said, "So do I have your blessings for this battle your majesty?"

And I replied "Go get them." He smiled, and the mirror stopped rippling. As I finished talking to him, I giggled like a small child, and went down stairs to hug my parents.

THE END.